A Candlelight Ecstasy Romance ™

"DAMN YOU!" SHE HISSED. "I SWEAR I'LL HATE YOU FOREVER!"

"No," he interrupted, the masculine humor fading at once. "You won't hate me. At least not forever!"

He moved, trapping one of her arms beneath the weight of his body and holding her other wrist above her head. His free hand went to the knot of her towel, but he made no immediate effort to undo it. He buried his mouth in her throat, and a slow, deceptively lazy trail of kisses began to work their way up toward her lips.

"Locke, please!"

"Please what, darling?" His tongue sampled the taste of her shower-warmed skin. "Please love you? But I do. And I will. . . ."

RELENTLESS ADVERSARY

Jayne Castle

Enjoy this book?
Trade it in!
Thousand of books at:
READER'S HEAVEN
207 West Market St.
Lewistown, Penna. 17044

A CANDLELIGHT ECSTASY ROMANCE™

Published by
Dell Publishing Co., Inc.
1 Dag Hammarskjold Plaza
New York, New York 10017

Dell ® TM 681510, Dell Publishing Co., Inc.

Candlelight Ecstasy Romance™ is a trademark of
Dell Publishing Co., Inc., New York, New York.

ISBN: 0-440-17290-X

Printed in the United States of America

First printing—March 1982

Dear Reader:

In response to your continued enthusiasm for Candlelight Ecstasy Romances™, we are increasing the number of new titles from four to six per month.

We are delighted to present sensuous novels set in America, depicting modern American men and women as they confront the provocative problems of modern relationships.

Throughout the history of the Candlelight line, Dell has tried to maintain a high standard of excellence to give you the finest in reading enjoyment. That is and will remain our most ardent ambition.

Anne Gisonny
Editor
Candlelight Romances

RELENTLESS
ADVERSARY

CHAPTER ONE

Handling Locke Channing had a lot in common with handling a loaded gun or, Kelly Winfield smiled to herself, an uncovered fencing foil. One must take great care to keep the weapon pointed away from oneself. Unfortunately the exercise was turning out to have all the deadly fascination of a duel.

It wasn't her fault she found herself in the dangerous situation, Kelly decided as the waiter poured wine for her and Locke. She had asked her boss for a weapon, and Helen Forrester had calmly given her Locke Channing. Instructions and cautionary advice had not been included.

Kelly had known the moment Marcie Reynolds had shown him into her office that both were needed.

"Well," she began as the waiter withdrew, "have you any ideas? Since you insisted on discussing this outside the office, I assume Forrester Stereo and Video has trouble."

Her soft, slightly husky voice was politely businesslike, but even Kelly could hear the faint ring of challenge buried in it. Annoyed with herself, she lifted the wineglass and sipped the fine Pinot Noir as she waited for Locke's response.

Over the rim of the glass his warlock eyes clashed with her silvery blue gaze. "What makes you think I invited you out to dinner solely to discuss the investigation?"

Kelly surveyed him with extreme caution. "Since your arrival three days ago you've scarcely emerged from the computer room. This afternoon you presented yourself in my office and told me I had to have dinner with you, that you didn't want to talk about matters in such sensitive surroundings. What else am I to think?"

"How about thinking the obvious?" he suggested in a drawl of metal and silk. Every time she heard it, that voice managed to ruffle Kelly's nerve endings. Deep, beguiling, and dangerous.

"I thought I was," she parried softly.

He smiled at that, and the smile was every bit as dangerous as the voice. It didn't reach the jade-green eyes.

"Do we have to go through this?" he asked almost gently.

"You're the one who invited me out to dinner to discuss your findings," she pointed out smoothly.

The jade eyes narrowed with barely restrained impatience. "You know what I mean," he murmured. "You've known from the beginning. The day I walked into your office we both knew that there was something important happening between us."

If you only knew how important, Kelly thought ruefully. *You have the power to ruin my comfortable new life, and so far you aren't even aware of it.* Her smile widened slightly with a mockery that was mirrored in the silver of her blue eyes. Egotistical, self-assured male that he was, Locke Channing assumed that the electricity that had flowed so unexpectedly between them was generated by a primitive male-female attraction.

Kelly read the intent that seemed to radiate from his lean, curiously graceful body and wanted to laugh. The electricity existed, true enough, but it was being generated on her part by a very pragmatic wariness that had nothing to do with physical attraction.

"You will have to forgive me for not being able to abandon all the rules of the game at once. I am accustomed to a more refined sense of play," she said lightly.

"You mean you're going to put me through all the masculine paces before you surrender?" he demanded grimly.

"Use that word again and I won't even give you a chance to jump through the hoops. You'll find yourself looking for other dinner companions before you've even paid tonight's tab!" Kelly's normally gentle, throaty voice was laced with the beautiful, deadly steel of a fencing blade.

"You don't like the term 'surrender'?" Locke taunted gently. "I suppose I could find an appropriately romantic euphemism, but why bother? That's what it will be, and we're both intelligent enough to call things by their proper names."

With a small well-concealed shiver Kelly realized that Locke probably was the kind of man who thought in such elemental terms. But, given the circumstances, she could hardly blame him. Wasn't she viewing the whole encounter as some sort of elaborate fencing match? A match in which her chief advantage lay in the fact that her opponent didn't know he was fighting a duel within a duel. And she must keep Locke thinking that the bout in which they were engaging was the superficially simple one of the ae-ons-old contest between a man and a woman.

He was right to accuse her of knowing something had happened between them on the day Marcie had shown him into her office, though. Kelly was willing to acknowledge privately her own uneasy reaction.

The pert, redheaded secretary had made the introductions, apparently oblivious of the way Kelly and Locke had been studying each other. Then, still chatting pleasantly, Marcie Reynolds had withdrawn, leaving them alone.

Kelly had managed the appropriate invitation to take a seat and Locke had politely accepted. But she knew she

11

had been staring at him, silently composing anew her thoughts and reactions for the dangerous bout ahead.

Locke Channing was not at all the sort of man she had hoped to find herself dealing with. He was, in fact, the type she had unconsciously feared to find herself handling. Feared, but until he had walked through her door, hadn't really believed existed.

She had tried telling herself it was her own guilt and fear of discovery that had made her see him as unexpectedly dangerous but she knew better. The art of fencing had long ago taught her to trust her instincts and she would only be kidding herself if she denied those instincts now.

He was thirty-five or thirty-six, Kelly had decided, coolly cataloging his outward characteristics in an attempt to view him in reasonable perspective. And the years had left the unmistakable mark of experience on the hard, unhandsome, and implacable male face.

It was there in the jade-green eyes too. The eyes of a warlock, Kelly knew, a warlock who automatically mastered his environment because that was his nature. But this time she would be the master, she'd promised herself. She must control the weapon he was or she would become the victim.

Long black lashes framed the warlock eyes, lashes that matched the gun-metal black of his hair. He had taken the seat by the window, and the weak early spring sunshine that had warmed the Bellevue, Washington, morning had revealed the merest hint of silver at the temples. The dark hair was thick and arrogantly unstyled. In the back it brushed the collar of the crisp white shirt he had been wearing.

The office-formal effect of the white shirt had been ruined then as it was tonight by the absence of a tie. Locke seemed to habitually wear his shirts unbuttoned at the throat, and the casual, brown corduroy jacket was his only other concession to businesslike attire. There was a supple quality to the slant of the broad shoulders under the jacket. It had been evident then and Kelly was acutely aware of it tonight. The smoothly muscled outline of his chest tapered into a flat, narrow waist and lean hips. The taut pull of dark slacks over his thighs drew her attention to the sinewy strength in him at odd moments.

A finely tempered weapon, Kelly thought again as she met his eyes across the table. She'd realized even as she'd studied him that morning that he had been summing up her features simultaneously. His gaze had been bold, blunt, and aggressive.

She knew what he'd seen. What she hadn't been prepared for was the slight narrowing of his glance after he'd finished the assessment. The small action had made her mentally search for the words to describe his attitude. When she'd found them, she'd been shocked at herself. Locke Channing had walked into the room and instantly viewed her as quarry.

At the realization she'd frozen for a split second. Then she'd taken a firm grip on her imagination. He couldn't possibly know. Not yet. And she must keep him from learning the truth. She must make certain he continued to see her only as potential male prey. It was far safer that way.

He couldn't have been overly impressed with his initial overview, Kelly had told herself, not fully understanding the look in the jade-green eyes. Her waist-length brown hair had been scrupulously braided and anchored in a neat coil at the back of her head. What she hadn't known was how the red-gold that was buried in it had been revealed by the overhead light. The center part provided a strict frame for the silver-blue eyes, straight nose, and well-marked cheekbones. It was not a boldly beautiful face. It was not even a quietly beautiful face. It was a face full of intelligence, humor, and strength, and Kelly was ruefully

13

afraid it probably didn't conceal the fact that she would be turning thirty in a few months.

Tonight she was wearing the gray suit she'd worn to the office. The nipped-in line of the jacket revealed her slender waist and small high breasts. The straight skirt shaped the full curve of hips and fell to her knees, hiding well-shaped thighs. She was five foot seven and wearing pumps, as she was tonight, Kelly stood nearly five foot nine. Not high enough to enable her to meet Locke Channing on a physically equal basis. The man must have topped six feet by an inch or more.

"If I make an issue out of the word 'surrender' tonight, you will, with typical warped male logic, assume you're on to something," Kelly said very sweetly, surveying the salad that had been placed in front of her. "And I really don't feel like tackling the task of restructuring your male ego this evening. So I will remind you instead that you presently work for me and I am here for a report on your progress!"

Locke's harshly etched mouth moved in an unwilling smile of appreciation.

"That's right, keep the hired gun in line," he growled softly.

"Is that how you see yourself, Locke?" she asked innocently.

"I think that's how you see me," he countered thoughtfully. "It was there in your eyes when I walked into your office three days ago. You've hired me to do your dirty work but you're wary of me. And rightly so," he concluded with an unsmiling outrageousness that was vastly annoying.

Kelly met the jade-green gaze with a cool, straight glare. "It's not you I'm feeling cautious toward, Locke. It's the whole situation. I'm going to look a little foolish if my guess is wrong."

"You're going to look brilliantly perceptive if it's right,"

14

he pointed out, hunting through his salad for the sliced mushrooms. "Helen Forrester is already enormously pleased to have you on her management staff. If you pull this off, she's going to think you're God's gift to Forrester Stereo and Video!"

"You seem to know Helen quite well," Kelly remarked aloofly, not liking the trend of the conversation.

"I worked with her husband a couple of years ago before he died. A business association, but a friendly one. She's done an excellent job of taking over the reins of Forrester Stereo. When you told her you wanted to call in outside help, she remembered me."

"I see." Kelly smiled slightly at the thought of the graying blond middle-aged dynamo who was her boss. Helen Forrester was proving to have the flair her husband had lacked in running a large business. Kelly hoped for her sake that Helen's son, Brett, would start demonstrating some of that flair soon too.

"Tell me something," Locke abruptly instructed, discovering another mushroom and forking it up with relish. "What made you decide to conduct the physical inventory of the warehouse?"

"Nothing overly significant," Kelly admitted. "Just a few discrepancies and anomalies. My main excuse to Helen for wanting the inventory conducted manually instead of relying on our computer printouts was that it would give us a good baseline for future control."

"I'm surprised you bothered," Locke observed dryly, one black brow lifting sardonically. "Most managers have an irrational faith in the accuracy of computer printouts."

Kelly smiled thinly. She couldn't very well explain her own skeptical attitude toward computer records. To do so would be to reveal her personal knowledge of how easily a computer could be manipulated.

"Old-fashioned inventories are a good idea now and then," she murmured dismissingly. "You must under-

15

stand that it wasn't a case of turning up vast quantities of missing stock. The discrepancies that appeared could easily be attributed to minor errors in either input or hardcopy documentation."

"But you wanted to be sure?"

"Yes. If it's more than that, we've got to plug the source before it becomes costly. If it's only a case of poor clerical work, then I want to know that too."

"Why didn't you call in the firm that installed and programed your computer hardware?" Locke asked curiously.

Kelly shrugged, her mouth quirking downward briefly. "I wanted an unbiased opinion. You know how those firms are, they claim to have provided all sorts of safeguards in their systems. They don't want to go looking for an obvious breach of internal computer security because it would make the programming look bad. Besides, I didn't have real proof. So I asked Helen if we could hire the services of a computer-security consultant. She gave me you."

"That's one way of looking at it," Locke said coolly. "I take a slightly reversed view of the situation. I like to think Helen handed you to me on a silver platter."

Kelly put down her fork with great care and let the chill show in her voice. "Need I remind you that as long as you're on this assignment at Forrester Stereo you're under my supervision? You're working for me, Locke."

He lifted his wineglass in mock salute, jade eyes gleaming. "You're determined to play the stupid game to the hilt, aren't you? Why? I wonder. Are you really so afraid of the ultimate ending or do you just like the hunt?"

"What I *like,*" Kelly retorted with icy emphasis, "is for the people who work for me to learn how to make concise, accurate reports when called upon to do so. I want to know what you've discovered in the past three days, if anything."

He sighed impatiently as the salad plates were removed. "Okay, business first. I don't think the problem is in the data base. It's difficult to be certain because a data base can be manipulated easily enough by someone who knows what he's doing."

Kelly swallowed but kept her expression calmly interested.

"But the kind of discrepancies you found would indicate something a little more sophisticated than a mere juggling of data. I'm going through the program now and checking it against the information you've provided."

"Looking for fingerprints in the Fortran?" She grinned suddenly.

"Something like that," he agreed dryly.

"Is the—er—cover story holding up with the computer-room staff?"

"You mean do they all seem to be buying the story that I'm at Forrester to consult on a new costing software package? Yes, I think so. At least no one's snuck up behind me, bopped me on the head, and then made furtive changes in the programming while I was unconscious."

"Does that sort of thing happen to you a lot on your consultations?"

"Don't look so delighted with the idea. No, it doesn't. By the time I get on the scene, the culprit is usually long gone. And some of them simply don't worry that much about being caught."

"Why not? Computer theft is a serious crime. It can mean thousands or millions of dollars to a company!"

"It might be big crime but it isn't being punished as such yet. The courts are just beginning to learn how to deal with it. It's often difficult to prove embezzlement or theft through a computer using traditional records and evidence. Those kinds of records don't exist in many cases. We are dealing, after all, with a system in which the paper trail so dear to the hearts of auditors is never created.

17

Most of the transactions are electronic impulses, not paper records."

Kelly nodded, knowing all too well how true that was.

"There's another reason the guilty parties often go unpunished," Locke added as the bucket of steamed clams was set between them. "And that's the undeniable fact that most companies, particularly banks that endure a lot of this sort of thing, don't want the bad publicity. They figure if people start worrying about the security of automated systems, they'll start worrying about the security of their money."

"So the offender is quietly dismissed?"

"Frequently that's how it's handled," Locke agreed. "People rarely take the same view of this sort of white-collar crime as they do of other types of crime. The use of the computer makes it all seem so impersonal."

"Any idea how much longer until you can pin down our problem?" Kelly pressed, helping herself to several clams. *And how much longer I'll have to fence with you?* she added silently.

He hesitated and then shrugged. "A day or two."

Kelly frowned, not liking the indefinite sound of the response.

"But I may be staying on longer than that," he went on smoothly.

She glanced up quickly. "Why?"

"Helen said something about sticking around a while and offering some advice on tightening up the security of the system in general so this sort of thing isn't likely to happen again."

"That's news to me," she retorted suspiciously. "Helen didn't mention contracting for your services beyond the present assignment."

"Don't worry, you'll get used to having me around," he promised silkily.

"Once you've solved my problem, I'll see to it that

you're handed off to another department," Kelly said with an outward calm she was far from feeling. She did not want Locke Channing hanging around Forrester Stereo any longer than was absolutely necessary. He was too smart, too observant, and he knew a hell of a lot more about computers than she did. She wished she could guess the likelihood of his stumbling across her secret. Well, it had been a calculated risk bringing an expert into the picture. All she could do now was defend and feint.

"Coward," he drawled, jade eyes mocking.

"Not at all," she contradicted politely, digging a clam from its shell. "But I do have other things to do at Forrester besides supervise outside consultants."

"Does it give you a feeling of self-confidence to think of us in an employer-employee relationship?" Locke inquired casually.

"Perhaps."

"You're too smart to waste time fooling yourself like that. Why not accept the inevitable?"

"I see nothing inevitable in the situation," Kelly shot back stonily. Dangerous, yes, but not inevitable.

"And even if you did, you'd still go on fighting, wouldn't you?" Locke said with sudden perception as he buttered a slice of sourdough bread. "You're so accustomed to winning, you can't conceive of the alternative."

"You're wrong," she said quietly with great depth of feeling. "I can conceive of losing."

"But not to me?"

"Not to you," she agreed.

"Or to any other man?"

"I'm a big girl now, Locke. At my age a woman with any sense doesn't want a win-or-lose situation. She wants an intelligent, mature relationship."

"So does a man my age who has any sense. Having the one doesn't preclude having the other, though. Your surrender as a woman doesn't imply your intellectual surren-

19

der, you know." His eyes narrowed. "Or don't you know how to separate the two?"

"You do, I suppose?" Kelly demanded with a little more sharpness than she had planned. She needed to play this very carefully, issuing her invitation to the attack with just enough realism to keep him from looking for the underlying duel.

"It will be my pleasure to teach you the difference," he promised softly.

Kelly stiffened slightly. "Have you spent the past three days planning my seduction?" she asked evenly, her silvery blue gaze focused on the dwindling pile of clams as she searched out another likely bite.

"No, I've spent the past three days working on the problem for which I was hired. It's the past two nights I've spent working on your seduction!"

"Your ego is most impressive. Does playing God with a computer give people like you the notion that you're invincible?"

"No, being a man who has discovered a need for a certain woman gives me the courage to enter the arena. I have the added advantage, of course, of knowing you're willing to engage in the battle. I saw that much in your eyes that first day. You can't blame me for hoping you would take the next step and realize the battle wasn't necessary."

Kelly felt the red flow up into her cheeks but managed to say tartly, "I don't see why one realization should follow the other!"

"It's simple enough," he returned easily. "If you're willing to acknowledge my pursuit to the extent of defending yourself, then you've as good as admitted I'm a threat. Having got that far, it's only a short step to realizing you wouldn't have perceived a threat unless you were attracted to me. If you're attracted to me, why fight it?"

"I suppose it's your training in computer programming

that has taught you to think in such a convoluted manner!" she snapped.

"It's a totally logical manner. Any self-respecting computer would be proud of me. Your thought processes are the ones that would short-circuit the machine. Are you going to eat that last clam?"

"Be my guest," she told him irritably.

"Thank you." He deftly removed it from the pot with the tongs.

Kelly watched him for a moment, blue eyes deepening slightly in color under the influence of the candlelight. Her fingers drummed idly on the white tablecloth while she considered her situation.

"What makes you so sure you want me?" she finally asked, unable to resist the question.

"Fishing for compliments already?" he said, glancing up with an unexpectedly boyish grin that made Kelly blink. "Maybe that's a good sign."

"I'm looking for rational explanations!"

He nodded. "How about love at first sight?"

"I said rational explanations, not science fiction! Besides, love at first sight is a female fantasy, not a male one."

"What's the male equivalent?" Locke demanded interestedly, green eyes laughing at her now.

"Desire or lust at first sight, I imagine," she told him bluntly.

"Well, I won't say I didn't experience that," he agreed slowly. "If I did say it, you'd have a right to be offended! But there's more to it than that."

"All of which was immediately apparent to you the instant Marcie showed you into my office?" she taunted, unwillingly remembering the leap into violent awareness her own senses had taken in the crucial moment.

"We spent several hours together, remember? But I didn't learn anything new during those hours. I merely

21

confirmed what I'd experienced during our initial meeting," he shrugged carelessly.

"Which boils down to you deciding that you want me," she retorted scathingly.

"You have to start somewhere," he smiled philosophically. "And wanting each other seems as good a place to begin as any other point."

"And if I don't agree?"

"That's your feminine way of telling me you want to make a fight of it. And if that's what you want, that's what you'll get. Never let it be said I denied my woman whatever she wanted!"

"You're quite incorrigible, aren't you?" Kelly whispered, lost in laconic admiration. "Do you always treat your female employers with such insolence?"

"Now you've moved from fishing for compliments to inquiring into the women in my life," he noted in satisfaction. "We're moving right along, aren't we?"

"If you say so. Personally I'm finding it hard to follow your train of thought!"

"You'll learn. How about dessert?"

"No, thanks," she said firmly.

"I'm with you. We'll wait until later."

Kelly raised a quelling brow but said nothing. His aggressiveness really was amazing, she thought with near-detachment. She'd met self-confident, egotistical men before but Locke Channing was proving to be world-class material.

It was all a veneer, of course. It always seemed to be that way with the men she encountered. Sooner or later the underlying weakness would surface, as it had with Brett Forrester and Ward Newlin.

Grimly she put the memories out of her mind as Locke politely held her chair. It wasn't that she couldn't accept the idea of a man having certain weaknesses as well as strengths, she told herself forcefully as they made their way to the door. But she was damned if she was going to let another male trade on her strengths to compensate for his own weakness. Not when he wasn't capable of offering the same deal in reverse.

But it would never come to that with Locke Channing, Kelly assured herself as they stepped out into the chill Washington night. With Locke she was engaged in a fencing match. Any weakness she uncovered in him was to be exploited in order to protect herself. And she was under no illusion that he wouldn't also be testing, feinting, and otherwise attempting to find her poorest line of defense.

She would not have to feel sorry for this man, Kelly thought suddenly, a rush of some heretofore unknown thrill pouring into her bloodstream. She need only keep in mind that he was an opponent.

"How long ago did you move to Bellevue?" Locke asked conversationally as he held the door of his black Jaguar for her.

"About a year ago," Kelly replied distantly.

"Where were you moving from?" he persisted just before closing the door.

"San Francisco."

"Quite a change."

"I haven't regretted it," she told him aloofly.

"But you'd rather not talk about it?" he hazarded dryly and slammed the door before she could respond.

"I'm a native myself," he went on cheerfully, opening the door on the other side and sliding behind the wheel. "Grew up here in the Northwest and went to school at the University of Washington over in Seattle. I probably never would have got down to San Francisco. Lucky for me you had the sense to move here!"

Kelly smiled politely in the darkened car but said nothing. She was too busy deciding how to handle Locke. The Jaguar sped through the rain-shimmered city with its sprinkling of high-rise buildings and on into the residential

23

neighborhoods perched on the edge of Lake Washington. In the distance, sitting in the middle of the lake, Mercer Island glittered with its necklace of expensive, shoreline homes.

"Where are we going?" Kelly roused herself from her reverie to ask, frowning across the distance of the front seat.

"Home for a nightcap naturally. Isn't that the usual procedure?"

"Only when the couple is heading for the woman's home. In which case you missed the turn!" she stated waspishly.

"Would you have invited me in if I'd taken you straight home?" he asked pleasantly.

"No."

"That doesn't leave us with much choice, does it?"

"Locke, I'm really not in the mood to play any more games tonight. I've had dinner and your report, along with a great deal of unnecessary philosophy, and I'm ready to call it a night," Kelly began determinedly.

"I hope you're not contemplating anything dramatic like leaping out of the car and screaming for assistance," he said. "We're almost there and it would be a pity if you got yourself soaked. It's going to rain again in a few minutes."

"Locke, whether you like it or not, there are rules to this game and you're not following them," Kelly said flatly, more annoyed with herself for having got into the situation than anything else. She didn't sense any genuine danger yet, only the potential for more combat.

"I know. I'm stepping outside the rules long enough to kidnap you. It's an old, established method of obtaining a woman," he chuckled, his strong hands shifting slightly on the wooden steering wheel.

"Perhaps among your relatives; certainly not among mine!"

24

"If the women in your family tree were anything like you, they probably wound up being the kidnappees more frequently than they'd like to admit. Women like you were born to fascinate men like me."

Kelly considered that for an instant, faintly intrigued. "Being fascinated makes you vulnerable," she finally warned softly, slanting a long silvery glance at his hard profile.

"I was wondering when you'd realize that."

He turned the Jaguar into a steep drive and parked it among the trees that surrounded the angular cedar-sided house. Then he turned in the leather seat to face her with masculine challenge, warlock eyes glittering.

"So come into my parlor little fly and we'll find out which of us is the most vulnerable." His hand went to the doorknob.

"One drink, Locke. That's it," Kelly said with sudden imperiousness, her fingertips moving to touch his sleeve in a silent bid for his full attention.

He glanced down at her hand and then back into her determined eyes.

"Whatever you say. Now that the kidnapping is an accomplished fact, I'm willing to step back inside the rules."

She believed him, Kelly realized. The only problem lay in guessing when he'd once again disregard those rules. But somehow that danger perversely heightened her own interest in the match.

CHAPTER TWO

It occurred to Kelly as she allowed herself to be led into the warm, solid cedar interior of Locke's home that she was making the tactical error of letting her opponent choose the grounds for the initial phases of the duel.

Well, she added with honest wryness, perhaps she hadn't exactly "let" Locke choose the setting. It had been more a case of having him ignore her objections.

"It's a lovely home," Kelly found herself saying in mild surprise, glancing automatically around the golden wood interior with its two story living room. Masses of windows framed the night-darkened lake with its glittering shoreline lights. A curving staircase led up to a second level on which a lofted den jutted partway out over the living room. A huge stone fireplace dominated one wall, and off to the side she could see the kitchen entrance.

"You mean not quite the sort of place you expected to find a computer type living in?" Locke teased, coming up behind her after closing the door.

"You said it, not me . . ." Kelly began, her mouth curving upward as she swung around to face him, and then she stopped in astonishment as her glance fell on the mounted foils on the wall over the dark couch.

The sight nearly stunned her. In one glancing blow it threw the whole match into a far more serious business. She was up against an adversary who *understood!* No! That was only her imagination at work. . . .

With an effort of will she tore her frozen glance away from the wicked sight on the wall and smiled a smile of dazzling brilliance. It was her best defense at the moment.

"Do you fence, Locke?" she murmured with a fair imitation of polite interest.

The warlock eyes flicked to the foils and back, and he said, equally casually, "A souvenir of my youth, I'm afraid. I did a little fencing in school."

"How interesting."

Kelly wandered over to study the quadrangular blades terminated at the point by a flat tip. "I, uh, was also exposed to it in school."

"Done much since then?" he inquired softly. She could feel his gaze on her back as she studied the blades. She also heard the probing behind the polite question. The room seemed alive with a strange tension.

"Oh, once in a while in San Francisco I got in a bout down at a club, but you know how it is. . . ."

"Same here. It's difficult to find the time and then to line up an opponent. It's not really a major sport in this area."

Kelly smiled again, her eyes still on the foils as she said very carefully, "Are you suggesting I have my seconds call upon yours?"

"Hardly necessary for a friendly meeting, do you think?" he drawled smoothly. "It's not as if a match between us would be over a question of honor, after all. If you like, I can set up something informal here in the living room. There's quite a lot of space once the furniture is out of the way."

"Perhaps sometime when we're both free . . ."

"Tomorrow night after work?" he pounced.

Kelly turned to face him, her expressive features full of humorous suspicion. "Am I being hustled by any chance?"

He grinned back unrepentantly. "Careful. I might per-

27

ceive being called a hustler as an offense to my honor. That would necessitate a match that might not be so friendly!"

"You're evading the question."

"Well, maybe I am setting you up a bit. Helen told me you fenced and I couldn't resist getting you here tonight so that I could show you how much we have in common."

"Does your desire to entice me include making sure I'll win?" Kelly eyed him with cool appraisal.

"Would you want me to throw the bout?"

"No!" The denial was automatic and vehement.

"I didn't think so."

Locke tossed her a knowing smile and turned to walk toward the kitchen. Kelly watched him for an instant, knowing now why his pantherlike grace had appealed to her senses. Unconsciously she had recognized the physical characteristics she admired most: the coordination and grace of a trained fencer. All the more reason for caution, she told herself, following him slowly. That deceptively lazy litheness could explode in a sudden burst of energy and speed capable of overwhelming an opponent.

"How," she asked aloofly, watching as he located a bottle of brandy and a couple of snifters, "did it come about that Helen mentioned fencing?"

He poured the brandy, not looking at Kelly. "After I'd spent those three hours with you going over the computer problem, I went back to Helen's office and told her I wanted to know everything there was to know about you."

"Locke!"

"Don't look so appalled," he advised, putting the brandy away and lifting the glasses. "Only a fool goes into a serious match without learning something about the adversary."

Kelly opened her mouth to protest and then shut it again, stepping aside to let him precede her back into the living room.

"I'm surprised Helen was so willing to discuss me with

28

you," she finally announced tartly as she obediently joined him on the couch.

"I was rather insistent," he murmured dryly, handing her a snifter. "I can be when the occasion warrants it. And I was fairly certain you'd make a fight of it, although I had to make an effort to talk you out of that this evening." He sipped the brandy and watched her intently.

"Has anyone ever told you that your audacity borders on the rude?"

"Never!" he assured her, settling back into a corner of the couch and continuing to rove her body with hooded eyes.

"Allow me to have the privilege, then." Kelly frowned her annoyance into the brandy snifter, cautiously inhaling the aromatic fumes.

"So far tonight you've called me a hustler and accused me of being rude. Any further insults to add to the list before I avenge myself tomorrow after work?"

"I'm sure something else will occur to me." Kelly was acutely aware of the fact that she had just tacitly agreed to the match. Locke was too. She could tell by the slow, satisfied smile shaping his hard mouth.

"Let me give you a few suggestions," he urged, sitting up with a smooth, gliding movement that somehow managed to include removing her glass from her hand. He set both snifters on the wide coffee table.

"Locke? What are you—"

She was in his arms before she fully realized his intention. "I only came in for the drink," she told him impatiently, bringing up her hands to wedge against his chest. "Let me go. I do not like the aggressive approach!"

"Pity. I have a feeling it's the only tactic that would work with you."

"Why, you arrogant, overbearing, insolent—"

"I won't say you're beautiful when you're angry," he

29

whispered a little thickly, his mouth only an inch above her own, "but you are sexy as hell!"

He pulled her close, his hands sliding up from her wrists to her shoulders and then around to envelop her stiffly held back. Furious now, Kelly turned her face aside, denying him her mouth.

He didn't fight for it, bending his head to find the taut outline of her throat instead.

"You said you were going to stay inside the rules!" she accused angrily, jolted at the shock of his lips on such a vulnerable part of her body. Her fingers closed into small fists against his shoulders.

"You can't expect me to apologize every time I lapse," he grated against her skin. "We'd both get tired of hearing me say I'm sorry. Especially when we both know I don't intend to change my tactics!"

Kelly didn't waste any more breath berating him. Deliberately she found the base of his neck with both thumbs and began to press steadily. The effect was immediate. He lifted his head at once, green eyes flashing with sudden impatience.

"Why, you little—"

He didn't finish the sentence, taking hold of both of her wrists and prying them away from his throat. "Where did you learn that little trick?" he growled.

"There are some men who don't respond to reason!" she flung at him, icy blue eyes chilling.

"You really are going to make a fight of it, aren't you?" he mused, scanning her flushed, angry face.

"I have no wish to brawl with you. Please take me home!" Kelly ordered haughtily, devoutly wishing her fascination with the duel had not overcome her common sense. It was obvious she should never have agreed to go out with Locke Channing this evening. All she could do now was recover to her on-guard position.

He hung on to her wrists, transferring them both into

one strong hand, and leaned forward, crowding her backward onto the cushions.

"I won't let you treat me like this!" she snarled, crushed under the weight of his hard leanness as he sprawled heavily across her.

"How are you going to stop me?" he retorted, manacling her wrists above her head and using his free hand to stroke the line of her jaw from the tip of her ear to her chin. She shivered at the light, exploratory touch.

"Damn you, Locke Channing! Who the hell do you think you are?" she raged, stunned and not yet believing her own helplessness.

"I'm your opponent, remember? And I'm going to win this engagement."

"No!"

But it was too late. Even as she tried fruitlessly to twist away from his grasp, Kelly knew it was useless. She was trapped between him and the cushions, unable to move more than an inch or two. She couldn't even free a leg. He had both of them anchored beneath his own.

"Lie still, you little hellcat. I'm not going to hurt you!"

"You already are hurting me!"

He didn't bother to argue further. With compelling, domineering aggression Locke covered her mouth with his own. Deliberately, ruthlessly, he forced apart her lips, holding her head still with his hand.

Kelly, struggling for breath against the combined effects of his crushing weight and mastering lips, stopped trying to fight and lay quite rigid. Instinct told her that Locke thrived on the challenge and he would only meet her resistance with increasing aggression.

She heard his groan of satisfaction and mounting urgency as he felt her passiveness. The plundering kiss became more persuasive and drugging, his tongue invading her warmth.

31

Kelly held herself in frozen suspension as his hand slid down her throat and inside the collar of her blouse.

"Don't you know," he husked against her mouth, his eyes flicking open to meet her defiant ones, "that the passive routine is just as useless as the outright struggle? What I want is a response, and you're not going home tonight until I get it."

"What you want is a surrender! You've already made that quite clear!"

"But I don't expect that much from you tonight, honey," he breathed on a note of humor as his fingers toyed with her top button. "Just a little response. A little warmth from your fire . . ."

He took her lips again and Kelly's eyes fluttered shut, knowing he had undone the button and knowing she could do nothing to stop him from going on to the next and the next.

But she cried out her protest, pointless as it was, when his fingertips found the soft, gentle curve of her breast. The exclamation was a strangely strangled sound, half blocked in her throat.

"Stop fighting me, sweetheart," Locke urged, his words thickening with masculine desire. His fingers began tracing slightly roughened patterns around the nipple he had found, and his kiss deepened with passion.

It wasn't a question of fighting him physically, Kelly knew with bleak realization. All she could do was pit her willpower against his, show him that her body was under her command, not his.

But even as she lectured herself she felt her breast swell at his touch, knew the sensuous tension of a tautening nipple. He was aware of the response at once, his hips arching intimately against hers.

"Can't you see how much I want you?" he grated pleadingly, ceasing the ruthless dominance of her mouth to begin stringing tiny heated kisses along her throat to the top of her breast.

"Why should your desires matter to me?" she charged tightly, and then spoiled the cold effect of the words by gasping as his tongue stroked her nipple.

"Because you're the only one who can satisfy them!" he almost snarled.

He shifted his weight slightly, pulling her blouse completely free of her skirt and pushing the silky material aside to expose her to his hungry gaze.

"You hardly know me!" she accused in a breathless whisper, horribly aware of the most vulnerable sensation she had ever known. Never had a man used his superior strength to hold her immobile like this while he took his time feasting on the sight of her.

"I knew all I needed to know about you within the first few minutes of meeting you, sweetheart," he contradicted softly, spreading his hand flat between the valley of her breasts and sliding it down to her stomach, which contracted at his touch.

"Did your dazzling perception also tell you that I'll never forgive you for humiliating me like this?" she gritted as his jade eyes lifted to clash with hers.

He lowered his head and briefly kissed the warm skin of her waist and then smiled down into her enraged eyes. "I'm not humiliating you, honey, I'm making love to you."

"You've got your terminology wrong. 'Rape' is the word you should be using. I doubt if you know the meaning of 'making love'!"

That, at least, seemed to get through to him. His dark eyes narrowed and the caressing fingers on her stomach halted for an instant.

"You think I would do that to you?" he rasped fiercely.

"I think it's pretty damn obvious that's what you're

doing!" she flung back, knowing she had just found a tiny weapon.

"No! You're going to want me as much as I want you," he promised, his nails lightly scoring the sensitive skin around her navel.

"Do I sound like I want you?" she dared recklessly.

"You're just afraid to admit the truth at this point, but you will before we're finished!"

"Famous last words! What happens if we finish and I still haven't admitted the 'truth,' as you call it? What will you do then, Locke Channing? Find another justification for what you've done?"

His hand went to her thigh under the hem of her skirt and he leaned forward to touch his tongue to the delicate area of flesh just above the waistband.

"If I make you mine tonight, there won't be any need for justification in the morning," he swore heavily.

She felt his fingers trailing upward in small exquisite forays, slick and tingling against the nylon of her panty hose, and Kelly drew in her breath. When she would have moved her legs in an effort to deny him what he sought, he trapped one ankle beneath his own. Once again she knew the dismaying vulnerability.

"You lied to me this evening," she managed, gulping air. "You aren't going to waste your time seducing me into surrendering, are you? You're simply going to force yourself on me! You don't need me for the kind of satisfaction you want. Why don't you go out and find a more willing woman? Or do you get some sort of perverted pleasure out of rape?"

"Shut up!" he ordered abruptly. "You're working yourself up into a panic."

"The one quality you're not lacking is nerve, is it, Locke?" she retorted bitterly. "You attack me, use your strength against me, and then accuse me of panicking! Sorry, but there aren't a whole lot of alternatives available to me. I assure you that when I'm free I'll find something more suitable like phoning for the police!"

"Stop it, Kelly!" he bit out, withdrawing his hand from her leg and gathering her close against him. "What's the matter with you, little vixen? There will be no rape and you know it!"

"No, I don't know it," she wailed into the material of his shirt as he pressed her head there in rough comfort. His hand stroked the length of her back now in long soothing movements, and she knew the passion in him was under control. "You've done nothing but provoke and taunt me all evening and then, as soon as you get me home, you attack me! How do I know what you'll do next? I was a fool to even have dinner with you."

"Well, at least you're not crying," he sighed. "All that feminine outrage means I haven't made a dent in your fighting spirit!"

"Is that what you were trying to do?" she hissed, her words muffled. The long languid stroking of his hand was unexpectedly pleasant and the heat of his body was inviting now that she no longer had to fear it.

He hesitated and then said wryly, "I had this theory, you see. . . ."

"What are you talking about?"

He cradled her against his chest, pulling her onto his lap as he sat back into the cushions. She sensed his smile as he rested his chin on her disheveled head.

"I thought I might be able to avoid a protracted skirmish by a quick, overwhelming rush of your defenses," he admitted.

"Of all the—"

"Hush," he commanded gently, pushing her face more thoroughly into his shirt so that her words were cut off ruthlessly. "No more names tonight. I figured that's all they were, you see. Defenses. I'm still inclined to think

35

that's all they are, to tell you the truth. I believe you want me every bit as much as I want you."

She stirred violently against him but was unable to get out the blistering words.

"I couldn't have been mistaken about the expression in your eyes three days ago or the excitement in them tonight, for that matter," he went on resolutely. "But I know you're intent on making a running battle of it and I'd just as soon get past all the initial feints and testing."

"You're wrong!" she got out.

"It wasn't only the challenge in your eyes, you know," he went on seriously, his fingers toying with the loosening coil of braided hair. "Everything else about you was calling out to me, daring me to make a move. I told you I'm fascinated by you. When I got you to have dinner with me tonight, I figured your acceptance meant you were willing to commence the battle. The one advantage I have is brute strength, so I decided to try using it."

Beneath her cheek Kelly felt one wide shoulder lift in a negligent shrug. "But it's obvious you're not going to let me get away with that tactic. Crying 'rape' was guaranteed to parry that attack," he concluded.

He let her lever herself slightly away from his chest, and she raised resentful, narrowed blue eyes.

"Keep in mind that there's a counter for every known attack!"

"Every fencer knows that, but not every fencer wins every time." He grinned unabashedly.

"The one surefire technique for not losing is to refuse the match!"

"It's too late for that," he whispered, voice deepening with conviction as he looked down into her wary face. "I've already thrown down the gauntlet and you picked it up when you agreed to have dinner with me this evening. I figure we'll call this evening's events the 'salute.' We are both now on our guard. Tomorrow after work we'll see how good your footwork is!"

She stared up at him, an inexplicable conviction taking hold that he was right. She couldn't refuse the match, although he was wrong about the reasons. For as long as he was working at Forrester Stereo she had to know precisely what he was doing and how much he was learning. Every moment he spent near the computer was another moment of risk. The tension of wondering how much he might have discovered would be unbearable. She had to maintain the contact, as dangerous as that was.

"You can't believe I'm stupid enough to see you again tomorrow night after what you pulled this evening!" she declared scornfully.

He smiled his dangerous smile. "How can you resist the idea of fencing with me? You know full well you're going to be seduced by the lure of demolishing me in armed combat!"

Kelly blinked in slightly appalled resignation. He was right, of course. The possibility of defeating him was incredibly tantalizing. Even if she didn't have her own reasons for maintaining contact with this man, the challenge of fencing with him would have been irresistible.

"You may have a point there," she agreed dryly, lowering her lashes to hide the speculative gleam she knew would be in her eyes.

"That's why I mentioned it before trying my short-circuiting attack here on the couch," he said, chuckling. "I wanted to have something to fall back on in case—"

"In case the brutality failed?" Kelly muttered irritably, cautiously beginning to search for a way out of his embrace.

"I didn't hurt you," he reminded her reproachfully, ignoring her scrabbling efforts.

She glared at him but didn't deign to dignify the protest with an answer. "Since you say you don't intend to follow

37

through with the manhandling approach, would you mind letting me go?"

He glanced down at the shadowy opening of her jacket and blouse, his eyes lingering on the curve of her breast. Again he smiled, this time with male challenge and a hint of pleading. It was an odd combination, and Kelly didn't trust it one inch.

"I'll take you home," he promised slowly.

"Thank you!"

"In exchange for one kiss freely given. . . ."

"Locke!" Kelly didn't know whether to slap him or scream her frustration aloud. "You've just said you wouldn't lower yourself to forcing your attentions on me," she reminded him vengefully.

"I won't. We'll sit here until we both fall asleep if you refuse the kiss, but I won't use force."

Kelly was about to rush into a string of protests and name-calling when she met his eyes in a straightforward exchange and decided he meant it. Unless she wanted to sit here in his lap until morning, she would have to meet his terms. Well, considering what might have happened this evening, the penalty didn't seem all that severe.

Gritting her teeth, she flung her arms around his neck without a word and ground her lips against his. He wouldn't have cause to complain about the fleeting, child-like quality of her forfeit!

He seemed taken aback momentarily by the forceful-ness of the embrace, but almost instantly his arms came around her, holding her in position for his response.

Kelly, intending a sudden, swooping, cold caress found herself caught gently, but firmly, against his chest, her breasts crushed softly as his lips parted before her violent onslaught.

Perhaps it was the unexpectedly submissive response of his lips that was her undoing. Or maybe it was the gentle-ness of his arms as he urged her closer to his heat and

38

strength. Whatever the reason, time seemed to suspend itself, while Kelly became intrigued by the inviting warmth of Locke's mouth.

There was no threat this time but a tantalizing, encouraging rejoinder. She found herself inside, exploring in intimate arousal. A part of her knew he was drinking in the kiss with surprising thirst, but her own reactions were dominating her mind at that moment. She couldn't take the time to be concerned with what he might be drawing from the embrace when her whole body was experiencing a thrilling sensation of wonder and astonished need.

She dug her fingers into his neck muscles with the luxurious movements of a cat kneading its paws. The instant response of his frame was the essence of excitement for her, and his groan of need and pleasure provoked her into arching her body against his.

As if that were a signal, Locke began to assume control of the kiss, thrusting his tongue past hers and into her mouth, as if searching for honey and almonds. His lips moved warmly, wetly on hers, and his fingers tracked up and down her back beneath the fabric of her blouse and jacket.

Kelly shivered and couldn't stop the tingling electricity that was uncoiling in her stomach. The kiss was literally taking her breath away, appealing to all her senses in a way she had never known before.

"Locke," she murmured against his mouth when he reluctantly broke that contact to nibble at the corners of her lips and the line of her jaw.

"You see, darling?" he husked as his hands probed beneath the waistband of the skirt. "You see how good it's going to be? I told you. . . ."

"No," she protested halfheartedly, trembling as his fingers clenched into the flesh of her buttocks. "You never told me! You attacked me!"

"You're the one doing the attacking now," he gritted

urgently, his teeth sinking almost painfully into her sensitized earlobe. "I hope you appreciate that I'm not fighting you the way you fought me a few minutes ago!"

"Such a good sport," she drawled in sultry humor.

"This is no time to laugh at me, sweet adversary!"

And he punished her with the elegant torment of his hands on her skin. Her reaction was instinctive. She twined herself more closely than ever, her legs twisting in need on the couch.

"My God! Did I ever have the wrong approach tonight! I should have just begun by asking for the kiss," Locke groaned as her fingers slipped down to his open collar and began unfastening the buttons of his shirt.

"You can catch more flies with honey than you can with vinegar," she quoted blissfully, her fingers winding through the crisp mat of hair on his chest.

"I don't know why I never paid more attention to that old cliché. Any others I should know about?" His mouth was moving down her throat and one hand was sliding around her waist to the small curve of her stomach.

She touched his thigh and smiled as she felt him tremble. "Probably, but I can't seem to think of them at the moment."

"Don't try to think," he advised. "Just feel!"

He had her jacket off now, and in another moment the blouse would be lying on the carpet beside it. Kelly moved in response to his manipulation of the fabric, and her eyes fluttered open for an instant.

It was long enough to catch sight of the mounted foils behind the couch. And for some reason they brought reality back in a rush.

"What's wrong, sweetheart?" he whispered, sensing her sudden tension.

"Nothing," she told him, deliberately pulling her chaotic senses together in preparation for the emotional and physical withdrawal. What had she done? What in the world was the matter with her?

"Kelly . . ."

She moved her head back against his shoulder and met the jade-green gaze with the sum of her will. With every ounce of energy she possessed, she curved her lips into a mocking smile.

"I've paid the forfeit. May I please go home now?"

"For God's sake, woman! How can you talk about leaving?" he growled. She could feel his whole body tighten, and the power in it should have frightened her but it didn't. It lured and beckoned and summoned. . . .

"You said one kiss and then you'd take me home," she reminded him sweetly, wondering what it would be like if he simply ignored her baiting demand. Whatever followed, she knew it would be unlike anything else she had ever experienced. And that alone was almost enough to make her stay.

"Stay until morning and we'll call the match a draw," he begged softly, coaxingly, green eyes like warmed emeralds.

"No." She shook her head lazily. "It wouldn't be a draw. It would be a victory—for you. I'm not about to make it so easy for you, Locke Channing!"

He stared at her as if trying to read her mind behind the sensuously hooded blue eyes. For a moment she thought she had indeed lost. The tension in the room was a living thing. She knew his instincts were riding high in that span of time. It would take very little for them to conquer the thin layer of civilization. Kelly lay very still in his lap and waited for her fate to be decided.

Abruptly it was over. With a movement that spun her sense of balance Locke set her on her feet, rising to stand beside her in a swift, fluid motion. For a split second his hands clasped her shoulders and he glared wryly down into her tense face.

41

"So we go back to the 'on-guard' position, hmmm? I was right. The only outcome you'll recognize is surrender. We'll see how gracefully you can lose tomorrow night."

He reached down to button her blouse, ignoring her efforts to do it herself. A slow, promising smile quirked his mouth.

And as he walked her out to the car, Kelly wondered if there was something unnatural or perverted about enjoying the kiss of the man who held the power to ruin her fine career at Forrester Stereo. What sane woman would willingly court disaster?

CHAPTER THREE

"Is Mrs. Forrester free for a minute or two, Carol?"

Kelly smiled down at the efficient, almost frighteningly organized woman who guarded Helen Forrester's office. Carol Winters nodded briskly, her dark eyes frowning a warning.

"Go on in, Miss Winfield. She's got a few minutes before her next meeting." Forty-three years old and with a wealth of experience at Forrester Stereo under her belt, Carol had no compunction at all about taking a superior attitude toward every member of the staff except Helen. No one dared walk into the president's office without checking first with the trim dark-haired woman at the outer desk.

"Good morning, Kelly, come on in. Coffee? It's okay to drink it this morning. Carol made it."

"Sounds terrific." Kelly grinned. "Don't get up, for heaven's sake, I'll get it." She helped herself to a cup from the pot and stirred cream into the brew. "You've got to break this habit of playing hostess in your own office, Helen. It just isn't done!"

Helen sighed, her gray eyes laughing up at Kelly as the younger woman walked forward to take a seat. She was an attractive woman in her mid-fifties, with short, styled blond hair that was silvering rapidly. On Helen it created an interesting effect, making the vivid gray eyes seem even more vibrant. A hint of matronly plumpness gave her a comfortable look that belied the astute mind and dynamic energy underneath.

"The result of too many years spent playing the role of the president's wife, I suppose!"

"Maybe you should find a nice, domesticated male and install him in your kitchen at home. If you had a househusband you might learn to feel more like a company president!" Kelly chuckled.

"Good idea but easier said than done. Unfortunately our society simply hasn't learned to train men properly for that sort of role. Pity, isn't it? I mean, when they're obviously so well suited for it temperamentally."

"Speaking of temperamental men," Kelly began, sampling her coffee with due caution, "I had dinner with the computer-security consultant last night."

"So I heard." Helen smiled. "Office grapevine," she added by way of explanation when Kelly lifted one brow interrogatingly.

"Of course," Kelly responded dryly.

"Now, there's a man who might *not* be temperamentally suited to housework," Helen opined thoughtfully, sipping her own coffee from a mug labeled BOSS, which Brett had given to his mother as a joke.

"I'm inclined to agree with you," Kelly began, about to launch into a description of Locke's findings so far.

"In fact," Helen interrupted with a rueful little smile, "I'm not sure what poor Locke would have done in life if he hadn't been lucky enough to be born in the computer era. Were you terribly bored last night, Kelly?"

"Bored!" Kelly stared at her boss a little blankly. "Well, no, not really, I mean we talked about the investigation. . . ."

"What else? From what I understand, computers are the only thing Locke discusses. Nearly drove his ex-fiancée crazy from all accounts!"

"Ex-fiancée?" Kelly waited with unexpected breathlessness for an explanation.

"Amanda Bailey. Her family are old friends of ours, which is how I happen to know the juicy details," Helen confessed with relish. Helen believed in maintaining a well-rounded interest in life. Being company president of Forrester Stereo hadn't destroyed her appreciation for good gossip, although Kelly had never known her to be malicious, except toward rivals.

"I see," Kelly murmured a trifle uncertainly. "Well, we didn't discuss his fiancée so I really don't know much about—"

"Oh, I can believe you didn't discuss Amanda! Locke probably doesn't even think about her. According to the poor girl, he barely seemed aware of the engagement when it was in effect, and the day she gave him back his ring he hardly looked up from the terminal long enough to tell her good-bye!" Helen was laughing now, gray eyes sparkling as she remembered the tale.

Kelly considered that for an instant, trying to imagine Locke being so blasé about his own engagement. "How—how long ago was this engagement?"

"It lasted all of two months and ended early this year. I'll have to admit that most of my information comes from Amanda's mother." Helen settled back in her executive chair and gazed thoughtfully out toward Lake Washington. "I expect it's the eyes."

"The eyes?" Kelly was beginning to have trouble following the conversation.

"Those marvelous green eyes. No woman could be blamed for thinking the man was capable of an interesting degree of passion. And with that black hair and those massive shoulders—"

"Helen Forrester!" Kelly finally exclaimed. "Are you by any chance trying to warn me about something?"

Helen looked sheepish. "Maybe I am, Kelly. Amanda

Bailey wasn't the first woman who discovered a romance with Locke Channing wasn't all she had thought it was going to be. From what I hear, the man has all the normal male appetites, but once they're satisfied, he turns to a computer for intellectual stimulation and companionship."

"Cold, hmmm?"

"Colder than the Puget Sound in January according to all reports. He uses those eyes as bait to catch an amusing little fish for dinner, but once he's satisfied his hunger, he loses interest. It's a mystery how Amanda got him as far as an engagement!"

Kelly hesitated a moment and then asked bluntly, "Why are you warning me, Helen?"

"Because he took the trouble to ask me a few questions about you, Kelly. And when I heard you'd had dinner with him, I got to worrying that you might be the next fish in line." The laughter faded from the eyes to be replaced by genuine concern.

"Do I look like a silly, unwary little fish?" Kelly asked gently, her mouth twisting in a sardonic smile.

Helen eyed her for a moment and then grinned. "No, my dear, you don't. Sorry about the interference. You're a big girl, aren't you? It wouldn't surprise me if this time Locke might discover he's trying to reel in a fish who's capable of biting back!"

"A female barracuda?"

"My favorite kind of manager! Okay, enough of the motherly hints. Tell me what Locke had to say about the inventory problem."

"Not much, actually. He expects to know more in a couple of days, I gather, after he's combed through the program. He also said something about staying on longer to examine computer security in general." Kelly waited. This was the real reason she'd come to Helen's office this morning. She needed to know how much longer the cat-

and-mouse game between herself and Locke would continue.

Helen nodded. "I suggested it after my conversation with him a few days ago. Don't you think it's a good idea? Especially if he turns up real problems in the inventory."

"His services don't come cheap."

"Prevention is always cheaper than the cure!"

She couldn't argue with that, Kelly acknowledged silently. It was beginning to appear that her nerves were fated to be strung out on tenterhooks for several days. Her mouth tightened unconsciously at the prospect. With a nod she set down her coffee cup and got to her feet.

"I just wanted to check in with you. I'd better be getting back to my office. Carol has your morning fully choreographed and I wouldn't want to be accused of upsetting the schedule."

"I'll see you later this afternoon, Kelly. I want to go over the figures on the contract with that Japanese firm. I'd like to add that line of speakers and turntables to our stock if we can come to terms with them."

Kelly summoned an agreeable smile and walked out, heading back to her office down the hall. She was almost there when Brett Forrester stuck his head around the corner of his door and called to her.

"Hey, Kelly! Is Helen in a good mood this morning?"

She turned and smiled a little distantly into gray eyes, which only recently had begun to assume some of the inner vividness of his mother's gaze. Curly blond hair and a well-trimmed mustache accented Brett's tanned good looks. The tan, Kelly knew, was from a salon that specialized in that sort of product. The blond hair was carefully styled by another expensive shop, and the designer suit fit the image Brett projected. Brett had excellent and expensive tastes. At thirty he was finally getting to a point where he could afford them.

"Her mood is fine, but Carol's got her on a strict timetable this morning."

Brett groaned. "I wanted to talk about our new marketing strategy for those video screens."

"Better talk to Carol first."

"I suppose you're right. You'd think a man would have better access to his own mother!" he added ruefully. "Well, if Carol's got her wrapped up for the morning, that will probably leave me free for lunch. Can I talk you into joining me?"

"Thanks, Brett, but I've got other plans."

He shrugged, accustomed to her refusals. Kelly wasn't sure why he still bothered to issue invitations. She had stopped accepting them several months ago.

"I heard you had dinner with that software consultant last night," Brett went on in a curious tone, his gray eyes watchful.

"The whole company seems to be aware of that!"

"Don't sound so annoyed. You know how office gossip is. Enjoy yourself?"

"It was business, Brett."

He didn't respond to that, merely lifting one blond brow in silent disbelief. "Whatever you say. My secretary tells me he's devoted to his job."

"He's certainly spending a lot of time in the computer room, but that's what Helen hired him for, isn't it? She wants an accurate consultation before investing in a more sophisticated costing package," Kelly told him aloofly.

"True, but I don't see why we even need to look into something more sophisticated. The computerized end of things around here is complicated enough!" Brett shook his head woefully. The wonders of the machine were a mystery to him, although he accepted the printouts as Gospel.

Which was rather amusing, Kelly decided as she smiled

and walked on down to her office. If one didn't mind a bit of morbid humor at this hour of the morning.

The faintly derisive smile was still in her eyes when she rounded the corner of her office and found Locke pacing back and forth in front of Marcie Reynolds's desk. Marcie threw her boss an apologetic, helpless smile.

"Mr. Channing would like to see you for a few minutes," the secretary began in relief, only to be interrupted by Locke's metal and silk drawl before she could finish the announcement.

"Where the hell have you been?" he demanded in obvious irritation, waving a sheaf of papers at her accusingly.

"In conference," she retorted coolly, acutely aware in every feminine bone in her body that there was no memory of last night in Locke's glittering green eyes. It reminded her of Helen's description of him. Cold . . .

"It's about time you got back, I've been waiting for fifteen minutes," he stated ungraciously.

Marcie winced and shook her head behind his back.

"Have you indeed?" Kelly retorted icily. "You could have saved yourself the wait if you'd made an appointment." With a quelling glance she reminded him which of them was in charge as she walked on into her office.

He followed, shutting the door behind them with a small violent little slam. Kelly ignored it and took her seat with an air of patient inquiry.

"Now, what, precisely, is so important that you had to drag yourself away from our computer?" she prompted quietly, searching his expression for any indication that he had stumbled onto something he shouldn't have. There was no sign of anything other than annoyance and, perhaps, a trace of satisfaction.

He flung himself into the chair on the other side of the desk and tossed the top paper from his handful onto the blotter.

"Does that address mean anything to you?" he demanded almost belligerently.

She picked up the paper, absently noting that Locke was in his usual uniform of unbuttoned shirt and corduroy jacket. His thick black hair was faintly ruffled as if he'd run his hands through it in exasperation. The green eyes were centered on her expectantly.

She glanced at the unfamiliar store name and address.

"No," she admitted calmly. "It doesn't."

"I think we'd better go look at it."

"Why?"

"Come on," he ordered brusquely, surging impatiently to his feet. "My car is in the lot outside. That area is somewhere south of Renton. It shouldn't take us more than forty-five minutes to get there."

"And another forty-five minutes to get back," Kelly pointed out with a touch of asperity. "I see no reason to go tearing off on a joyride when I've got enough work to do as it is!"

"This is important," Locke proclaimed, swooping around the desk and reaching for her wrist. He tugged her to her feet and had her halfway out the door before Kelly could dig in her toes.

"Does this have something to do with—"

"Yes," he interrupted unceremoniously, sweeping her past Marcie and on down the hall toward the elevators.

"Locke, I'm quite capable of keeping up with you. There's no need to make a scene like this. Marcie looked as if I were being kidnapped!" She bit her lip, wondering if the word would remind him of last night.

If it did, Locke gave no indication of it. Inside the elevator he released her to punch the lobby button and then leaned back, arms folded across his chest.

"If I'm right, I think I've found the source of the inventory discrepancy problem," he announced, glaring into the middle distance. Kelly had the distinct impression he

50

was hardly aware of her except as a necessary witness for whatever it was he had to show her.

Not the most flattering stroke for a woman's ego, she acknowledged with an inner grin, coming as it did after last night, but, thanks to Helen, it didn't come as the shock it might have been.

Five minutes later the black Jaguar was moving swiftly down the freeway that circled Lake Washington, headed for the southern end.

They passed one of the many aircraft engineering and manufacturing plants that dotted the area and contributed so heavily to the economy, and then swept on with a silent Locke at the wheel.

Kelly kept her peace until he exited the freeway and began heading into the countryside.

"There's a map in the glove compartment," he said briefly. "See if you can find the street."

Stifling a sigh, Kelly pulled out the large book map that covered the area and hunted through the index. Briskly she gave directions.

After a few more turns Locke slid the car to a halt in front of an obviously out-of-business storefront.

"Well, there it is," he said in cool satisfaction.

"The address?" Kelly frowned at the abandoned building. "I give up. What's the significance?"

"For the past six months Forrester Stereo and Video has been shipping some very nice stereo components to that shop. Not a lot, I would imagine, since you didn't find a lot missing, but it probably would have gone on indefinitely."

He twisted in the leather seat, one hand resting idly on the steering wheel, and grinned at Kelly. For the first time she had the feeling he actually recognized her.

"And the beauty of it is that the computer was programmed to ignore any reference to that address whenever someone asked it for a printout of current accounts."

"You mean someone phoned in the orders, the computer dutifully processed them and then created no record of the transactions?"

"Right. The components go to shipping and a truck drops them off here. I expect someone is available to receive them and everything would look normal as far as the driver was concerned. Everything was normal as far as the computer was concerned too. This particular account simply never got invoiced."

Kelly heard the professional admiration in his voice and smiled. It was ingenious. Certainly a lot more sophisticated than her own attempts!

"I told Helen I thought you were a little overpriced," she confessed wryly, "but I'll have to admit you earned your fee. This could have gone on indefinitely. I suppose whoever's doing this has a nice little income coming in from the sale of stereo components. Which brings up the logical question—"

"Of who's doing it?" he concluded with a thoughtful nod. "I have a theory on that."

"You're talking about someone capable of tampering with the original software package that was programmed into the computer when Forrester bought it," Kelly mused. "Frankly I don't think we have anyone on our staff who could do that. We don't have any use for full-time programmers. Our people just access the terminal for routine inquiries and reports."

"I think it *was* part of the original programming!"

"You mean someone from the firm we bought it from originally?"

"Uh-huh. I'll make some phone calls this afternoon." He turned in the seat and switched on the ignition. "Come on, let's get some lunch. We can lay out the whole mess for Helen before four o'clock."

Kelly agreed a little distantly, her mind plunging ahead to her own future. Having found the solution to the problem she had asked him to investigate, Locke would now have no specific focus for his work. Thanks to Helen's desire to tighten up the security of the system, he would have free reins to continue exploring the machine and its software. How much longer could her own luck hold out?

Over lunch at a surprisingly excellent restaurant specializing in pasta Locke elaborated on the intricacies of the scheme he had uncovered. Kelly let him talk, her thoughts turned inward as she listened with only a small portion of her attention.

"I'll pick up some steaks and a bottle of wine," she suddenly heard him say. "We can have dinner after the bout. Are you any good in the kitchen?"

"I beg your pardon?" It took an effort of will to realize Locke was talking about their scheduled fencing match. She could have sworn he'd forgotten it.

"It doesn't matter," he murmured magnanimously. "Between the two of us I expect we can put together steaks and a salad."

She met the flaring green eyes with a distinct sense of shock. Just like that it was all there. Somewhere between the salad and the ravioli Locke had remembered everything. The emeralds of his warlock gaze were once again glowing, and if there had been any doubt in her mind about his memory of last night, it was shattered on the instant.

For the first time since her conversation with Helen that morning, Kelly understood why Amanda Bailey might have lost patience with her fiancé. It was disconcerting, to say the least, to have a man switch gears so fast. It was bound to make a woman wonder how deep his passion really went.

Of course, Kelly reminded herself chidingly, she was hardly in the same boat as Amanda had been. After all, that poor woman had probably hoped Locke was in love. Kelly had only inspired desire in him. But if he'd gone from loving fiancé to cold, calculating computer expert with the same abruptness he was displaying in reverting from that to woman-hungry male . . . Kelly felt a tiny stabbing shiver. Somehow it all made him seem so much more dangerous.

But there was no denying that the potential danger was a good deal more intoxicating than the immature weakness she was so accustomed to from the male of the species. Late that afternoon, as Kelly tossed her mask and fencing jacket into a duffel bag, she wondered again if there was something wrong with her for finding the danger attractive.

"What's the bottle of wine for?" Locke demanded interestedly as she opened the door to him. His eyes swept her casual attire of jeans and electric-blue velour top, which seemed to accent the silvery hue of her eyes. "Don't tell me you're expecting to pay me off with that when you lose!"

"As I don't intend to lose, I'm certainly not worrying about awarding you a prize! This is for dinner. You said you were going to pick up steaks and wine. Well, here's the wine." She smiled at him brilliantly, her whole body aware of his intent regard. When he *did* turn on the desire, it appeared with a vengeance, she thought grimly.

"Fair enough," he agreed, picking up her bag and foil and leading the way out to the waiting Jaguar. "That does bring up the issue of tonight's trophy, however . . ." he began tantalizingly.

"Trophies aren't needed in affairs of honor. Only winning counts," she reminded him bluntly, sliding onto the leather seat and flicking his lean length with an assessing glance.

Dressed in a black turtleneck sweater and jeans, his gun-metal hair stirred by the brisk evening wind, which was bringing in a storm from the Pacific, Locke resembled a sorcerer with more than just his eyes.

"You're determined to view tonight's engagement in the traditional sense?" he drawled.

"Aren't you?" she countered, lowering her lashes to hide the faint gleam of excitement.

"Something tells me we both got into fencing for the same reason," he growled softly and slammed the door.

"You certainly managed to impress Helen with your sleuthing this afternoon," she began in a determinedly conversational voice as he slid behind the wheel. "She's convinced you ought to stay on now and give us the full benefit of your talents in the computer-security field."

"You aren't so convinced?" he inquired blandly, pulling away from the expensive apartment complex perched so that it overlooked a quiet bay on the lake. One of these days Kelly planned to buy, but for now she was enjoying apartment life.

"I'll admit you looked pretty good this afternoon coming up with the name of the guilty programmer!"

"Luck." He shrugged modestly. "A few phone calls put me in touch with someone I know who once worked for the firm. He told me the guy had been dismissed several months ago for suspicious causes. Since that was the programmer who'd worked on your project, it must have been him."

"Helen's turning it all over to the police. They'll stake out the closed storefront if the computer receives another order for that address."

"Helen's not going to be content to simply plug the leak and forget about it?" Locke asked very gently.

"Helen doesn't like being ripped off." Kelly smiled bleakly, not looking at him. "If he's caught, she'll prosecute."

"That's the feeling I got from her too. Well, now that I've programmed the machine to print out reports on orders received for that address, we'll know if another attempt is made."

"We?" Kelly prompted deliberately.

"Oh, I expect I'll be around for several more days," he said obligingly. "It will take me at least that long to assess the system completely."

Kelly couldn't argue with him: she didn't know if that was reasonable or not. How long did it take to analyze a computer system for weaknesses? But perhaps the worst was over. If Locke hadn't turned up anything threatening during his initial search, maybe she was safe. From now on, after all, he would be looking at generalities, not particulars.

"I'm not the only one who came out of this looking good," Locke went on after a moment of quiet. "As I thought, Helen's opinion of you has risen even higher, if that's possible."

"It was only chance that made me suspicious," Kelly said dismissingly.

"Have you had a lot of experience with computers?"

"Very little," she told him shortly, searching mentally for a way out of the conversation. "How long has it been since you've done any fencing, Locke?"

He threw her a quick, speculative glance. "Wondering if I'll be an easy target for you?"

"I take it you're not going to tell me," she returned blandly.

"A little uncertainty in one's opponent is always valuable," he grinned smoothly.

If he only knew just how much uncertainty he had brought into her life, Kelly thought feelingly.

By the time Locke had parked the Jag in his drive under the trees, Kelly could feel the adrenaline already pouring into her bloodstream. The need to test herself against this man was almost physical in nature. It was as if winning on the fencing strip somehow increased her odds of holding him at bay in other, more critical, areas.

She knew he was psyched up for the match too. Kelly

wasn't sure exactly how she was aware of his intent interest in the bout, but her senses were alert to every nuance of the situation and they assured her he was riding the same strange high as herself.

The furniture had all been pushed aside and the stylish, geometrically patterned area carpets had been rolled up along the wall. An imaginary fencing strip stretched across the front of the living room parallel to the full-length windows.

Locke's eyes were on Kelly's profile as she surveyed the preparations.

"Scared?" he whispered softly.

"Should I be?"

"Maybe a little," he conceded laconically. "You're going into combat with an opponent you know little or nothing about, aren't you?"

She turned her neat head to eye him coolly. "The same applies to you."

"That's debatable," he said evenly. "I've never seen you fence, but I do know a lot about you."

"No more than I've learned about you, surely?" she invited challengingly.

He smiled and said nothing. Hands resting on his lean hips, he swung an assessing gaze along the area prepared for the bout and then nodded briefly.

"I think we're both ready. You can change in the bedroom at the top of the stairs. I'll use the other one at the end of the hall."

Without a word Kelly lifted her duffel bag and headed for the winding wooden staircase. The level of excitement in her veins seemed to surge with every step. He followed silently, pointing out the room she was to use before retreating to another one farther down the hall.

As soon as she stepped inside, Kelly realized she had been assigned to Locke's own room. She glanced around, wondering with a sense of cool speculation if it had been a subtle psychological tactic on his part to have her change in an atmosphere heavily imbued with his presence.

But accusing him of such a move would be to give him more credit than Helen seemed to feel the man should have for sensitivity, she decided wryly, plopping the duffel bag down onto the wide bed with its thick down quilt.

Her eyes moved restlessly around the room as she pulled on the white trousers and high-collared protective fencing jacket. It was definitely a man's room, but not a cold one. The thick solid cedar walls lent warmth up here just as they did to the lower portion of the house. A blazingly designed area rug in black and red went well with the sleek modern furniture. The lines were strong and masculine but comfortable. Wide windows took full advantage of a partial view of the lake.

Slipping on the white shoes, Kelly finished her preparations, then stood in front of the mirror to draw on the glove. Her own blue eyes stared back at her, very silver and glowing with an inner exhilaration that couldn't be hidden. She was ready. She picked up the mask.

Kelly came silently down the stairs to find Locke waiting for her, foil and mask in hand. The jade-green eyes swung toward her the moment she appeared on the landing and followed her every pace as she came forward.

Without a word she closed her gloved fingers around the familiar handle of her foil and took up a position opposite Locke. The sensation of controlled power flowed through her body, and the knowledge that Locke was experiencing the same feeling added another dose of stimulation.

"There's nothing quite like it, is there?" Locke asked in a voice of cool silk, raising his weapon in formal salute.

"No," she whispered, echoing the traditional salute. "There isn't."

And there wasn't, she reiterated silently to herself as they slipped on the fencing masks. They had just stepped back into the past to confront one another across a stretch of grassy field beneath the cold light of dawn.

But for some reason tonight the fantasy was even more powerful for Kelly. She was facing a dangerous opponent who didn't yet know the full extent of his own potential menace. Winning suddenly became very important.

CHAPTER FOUR

There were two qualities necessary to make a good fencer, Kelly knew: instantaneous judgment in the heat of combat, and speed. With those, combined with a supple strength and stamina, a fencer became dangerous indeed. It didn't take Kelly long to realize Locke had it all. She was up against an excellent fencer, one who was better than herself.

She acknowledged the situation immediately and didn't waste time berating herself for having accepted the challenge. Even the best fencers made mistakes or misjudged distances and opponents.

It wasn't that Locke rushed to overwhelm her, but Kelly found herself defending almost immediately. She knew he was watching her reaction to his feints, gauging her preference for certain parries, and she was glad of having had instructors who were adamant about not telegraphing one's movements with one's hands.

Realizing the strength in his wrist, she carefully engaged the blades foible to foible, knowing pressure could be more easily neutralized at the weaker tips of the weapon. The entire blade could function as a lever with the hand being the fulcrum. If she allowed Locke to engage blades near the stronger base of the foil, he would have been able to use his superior strength against her.

The basic movements of advance, retreat, and change of guard were carried out in deadly silence, each fencer waiting for an opening. Coolly Kelly tried to use her retreats to deceive the distance, forcing her attacker to close the gap. It was a basic defensive tactic for a weaker fencer, but it couldn't be used indefinitely. Constant defense never produced a scoring touch. Sooner or later she would have to attack.

Both stuck to deceptively simple plays; straight thrusts, disengages, and cutovers were varied with beats, opposition, and occasional two-movement attacks. There were more complicated maneuvers in a fencer's repertoire but the advance planning required often made them self-defeating under the tension of combat.

Slowly Locke began to build the pressure against her, seldom using the same tactic twice in succession. He followed her retreat but did not advance aimlessly into her point. He kept his distance, displaying a satisfying respect for her blade.

Kelly hardened her defense, watching for an opening. Attack was followed by parry and riposte in a centuries-old game where losing had once meant death or injury. Kelly felt the single-minded intent emanating from Locke as if it were a palpable force. His fencing was aggressive and graceful, and he gave no quarter.

And then, quite suddenly, she tried an attack begun from complete immobility, and surprised Locke in the preparation of his own attack. He avoided it, but the action took him into retreat, and Kelly began to press the small psychological advantage.

The excitement of going on the offensive flowed through her. She sensed his new wariness and moved to increase it. Kelly knew her speed was increasing now as she warmed to the combat. Finding an opening at last, she moved into the attack with precision and confidence. Her body slid expertly into the lunge, trailing arm snapping vigorously behind her,

Locke defended swiftly, barely denying her the score,

but already Kelly was recovering with spring and litheness. She recovered forward, pressing the attack still further.

With that action the play became more even. Kelly still found herself relying heavily on defense but she knew now she had a decent chance of holding her own—and Locke must have known it too.

It was he, however, who brought the first phrase to a decisive close with a simple beat-lunge attack that drove the tip of his covered blade firmly against her jacket.

Acknowledging the hit, Kelly stepped back, catching her breath for the next phrase of the bout. They paused for a short rest and Locke lifted his mask. Silently Kelly followed suit, meeting his eyes across the distance.

"You're good." He smiled easily, jade gaze raking her face. "You nearly had me a couple of times."

"Nearly isn't good enough," she reminded him, aware of the perspiration on her forehead. Locke didn't look as if the match had yet begun to tire him.

"Perhaps during this next phrase," he suggested encouragingly, his smile taunting.

"It will be my pleasure," she assured him as they once again brought the foils up in salute.

"You realize, of course," he said quite neutrally, "that I can't afford to let you win."

Something in the evenness of his metal and silk voice alerted her.

"Trying to use a little psychological warfare?" she mocked as they slipped on the masks.

"I'll use whatever it takes," he agreed as they went into the on-guard position.

"It won't work," she assured him.

"No? How about this: I know all about your little cat-walk through the data base a few months ago."

Kelly froze, her clear, calculating, strategy-oriented mind thrown into complete chaos at the simple words.

"You see?" he murmured softly. "You're suddenly an undefended target." He moved forward in lazy offense, and Kelly retreated without thinking, her mind on his shattering comment.

Desperately she forced her mind and her nerves to regroup.

"When did you find out?" she asked coldly, determined not to let him see how much turmoil he had created. But she was very much afraid he already knew.

"Yesterday, when I went back for another look at the transactions that had been going on around the time of one of the unrecorded shipments," he told her offhandedly.

"I had nothing to do with the theft!" she gritted defiantly.

"I know that. You were content just to shift some rather large sums of money around, weren't you?" He executed a rapid change of engagement to the high inside line by passing his blade under hers and forcing her to engage in quarte.

"No money was stolen!" she snapped, covering the target area he sought.

"I spent this afternoon trying to figure out exactly why anyone would want to play with the data the way you had been playing with it."

She retreated as he tried a feint disengage. He was going to find this match a walkover, she realized disgustedly. She could no longer concentrate as completely as would be necessary to defeat him.

"And I couldn't come up with very many reasonable answers," he concluded, forcing her back again.

"I'm glad something in the whole mess was beyond your ability to decode," she shot back bitterly. She was tiring rapidly now and knew he was beginning to play with her. The knowledge filled her with self-disgust.

"There's a lot about you I have yet to decode," he

agreed, deliberately opening a line in an invitation to the attack.

Kelly accepted heedlessly and found him more than prepared for her lunge. He took her blade with his own, maintaining contact and using his superior strength to force her foil outside the limits of the target. A split second later his explosive response brought him another scoring hit.

Kelly backed off, lifting the mask away from her damp face and using the back of her sleeve to wipe her forehead. Across the room Locke removed his own mask and the glittering warlock eyes pinned her with the look of the hunter.

"I'm afraid your psychological warfare is going to be successful, after all," she admitted harshly. "I don't think I'm going to be able to give you much of a contest this evening."

"Does it rattle your confidence that much to know I found out about your maneuvers with the computer?" Locke asked with cool interest, setting his foil down as she did the same.

She drew a deep breath, letting her heart return to normal, and tried to think. Mentally she was again fencing with him.

"How did you find out?" she asked almost uncaringly, standing very still and watching him through narrowed silver-blue eyes.

"The computer recorded the 'corrections' you were making to its data base. The corrections always carried the same identifier. Your password was the one being used the most consistently when sums of money were juggled."

"I see." She shrugged, her mouth tightening. "I told you I didn't know very much about computers."

"Enough to realize that you could go in and modify columns of numbers to make them add up properly, it would appear," he countered.

"It seemed a logical way to handle matters," she sighed. "As you said, the computer leaves very little in the way of a paper trail. . . ."

"If it makes you feel any better, I think you would have got away with it indefinitely if you hadn't called in someone to check out your security problem. Did you realize how dangerous such an action was?" Locke inquired almost mildly.

"I knew there was a risk involved, but since I didn't know very much about the inner workings of the machine, I couldn't judge the extent of the danger." Kelly met his eyes with a straight glance. "In any event, I didn't have much choice. I couldn't solve the inventory problem on my own. I knew enough to realize I needed professional help."

"A calculated risk," he said, nodding with surprising approval. "You just couldn't quite calculate the exact dimensions of that risk. No wonder you looked at me with such wariness the first day. Have you been sleeping nights lately, wondering when I was going to discover the facts?"

Kelly's mouth twisted wryly. "Actually I'd begun to hope you might not find out anything at all. You gave no indication yesterday. . . ."

"I wanted time to think about the possible ramifications of your involvement in such an affair," he said quietly, unfastening the row of buttons along the side of his fencing jacket. "And I wanted to solve the inventory puzzle first. I figured you probably weren't involved in that or you wouldn't have called in someone to analyze the problem. You would just have made the—er—appropriate 'corrections.'"

She watched him warily, trying to assess his mood. He didn't seem outraged or angry or even disgusted. Instead there was a faint air of concealed triumph, determination, and calculation. What was he thinking?

"I suppose you have a reason for telling me of your brilliant sleuthing at this particular point in time?"

"Naturally. I fully intend to use the information, but you know me well enough, I think, to have guessed that." One black brow raised sardonically. He hadn't moved, still watching her from across the distance of the room.

Kelly felt as if she were in the presence of a large cat who was biding his time before the final spring. It was difficult, she found, to accept the total defeat Locke Channing had unloosed. She wasn't accustomed to losing. But the risks had been there from the beginning and she had accepted them.

Nevertheless, she discovered grimly, there was a certain double impact in the way he had done it tonight by combining his victory over her in the matter of the computer with another in fencing. She felt breathless and cornered.

Lifting her head proudly, she stared at him, eyes full of ice and snow. "You're going to go to Helen with the information?"

"Shouldn't I?" he demanded aggressively. She knew he was waiting to hear her try and argue him out of it.

She sucked in air, realizing she would have to try to do exactly that and it galled her to step into his trap.

"You're a friend of hers," she began slowly.

"Not a close one," he remarked, surprising her.

Kelly frowned. "And I'm sure you have your professional ethics to maintain."

"I'm not a fanatic about them," he stated evenly, raising a hand to carelessly thrust the dark hair back off his forehead. The green eyes never left her face, and she could sense the coiled tension in him.

"What if I told you that going to Helen would only upset her and there is no crime to report anyway?"

"I'm listening."

She threw him a stony glance, uncertain of his meaning.

"Are you telling me, by any chance, that you're open to a bribe?" she hazarded dryly.

"Are you offering one?"

"No. I don't have anything with which to bribe you," she shot back scornfully.

"Don't you?"

"Would you mind very much if we cut out the cat-and-mouse business?"

He hesitated as if thinking over the request. "Answer a couple of questions first and then I'll tell you whether or not I'll cut out the fencing."

She inclined her head once in a regal acceptance of his terms.

"Was it you who fooled around with the data base or was someone else using your password?"

"I'm quite guilty," she informed him calmly.

Something flickered in the jade gaze, but she couldn't decipher it.

"Did you embezzle from Forrester Stereo?" The question was clipped and cool.

"No."

"Then why—"

"That particular question I don't intend to answer," she interrupted brusquely. "I will only give you my word that no money is missing from Forrester's account."

"You must have had a reason for all those changes," he began, sounding faintly irritated.

"I did. The reason has been taken care of. No one's been hurt. And you needn't bother with any more questions along this line. I'm not going to answer them," she snapped crisply.

"Lacking a reasonable explanation from you, I probably should go straight to Helen," he pointed out.

Kelly swallowed. "I'll resign on Monday if that will satisfy your sense of justice."

His jaw hardened and he walked slowly toward her, coming to a halt a foot away.

"You'd resign over this rather than explain yourself to me?" he growled, one hand snagging her chin and holding her face very still.

Kelly nodded.

"What if I said I'd go to Helen in any case?" he went on grimly.

"You mean whether or not I resign?" she whispered, trying to shield the tumult he was causing in her mind as she contemplated that.

"Yes."

"You don't give an inch, do you? What is it you want, Locke? You've implied there's a way out of this. . . ."

"There is." He smiled challengingly, provokingly. "It will be interesting to see whether the escape clause is more acceptable to you than having Helen find out someone's been tampering with her financial data."

"Go on," she charged forcefully, holding his gaze bravely.

"You don't lack nerve, do you, woman?" he mused.

"I think you would crush me if I did."

"That's not true," he said gently. "But I probably would handle you a lot differently."

"Are you going to tell me your solution to the situation?" she asked tersely.

"It's simple enough. Marry me and I'll go back into the computer and wipe out all your little paw prints."

"Marry you!" Dumbfounded, Kelly could only stare up into the implacable face of her nemesis.

He waited in hard silence, watching the play of emotions across her face.

"You don't lack nerve either, do you, Locke Channing?" she muttered incredulously.

"Fencing still requires courage, even these days when

death isn't the ultimate penalty for losing," he reminded her whimsically.

"You think marrying me will be like entering a fencing bout?" she rasped, trying to assimilate what was happening.

"Initially, yes," he confirmed flatly.

Kelly stood transfixed a moment longer and then stepped firmly out of his reach. He didn't follow. From three feet away she glared at him.

"All right, Locke, let's have the whole thing out in the open. Why should you be willing to offer me this particular escape?"

"I made up my mind to marry you that first day when I walked into your office and found you waiting for me with such cool challenge in those lovely blue eyes. If this mess with the computer hadn't popped up so conveniently, I would have bided my time a bit longer before asking you. This way things are moving a little faster than they would have otherwise," he explained casually. "But the end result will be the same."

"You seem quite certain I'll take you up on your generous offer," she noted scathingly, wondering what was wrong with her pulse. It had begun to pound with the primitive fight-or-flight reaction of the female to the male. She knew, even as she despised the knowledge, that her body's reaction to Locke's challenge was elemental and very feminine.

"I don't think you have much choice." One broad shoulder lifted in an easy shrug, but the green eyes were glowing with aggressive demand.

"Aren't you taking a bit of a risk?" she taunted deliberately. "Marrying a woman of uncertain ethics?"

"Like I said," he drawled. "I'm not a fanatic about business ethics."

"What about other kinds?" she pressed bluntly.

"If you even contemplate cheating on me with another

man, you have my promise I'll bring you back in line the way men used to accomplish that trick in the days when the swords weren't blunted at the tip!"

"Threats already, Locke?" Kelly gritted sharply, a portion of her analytical mind informing her he meant every word.

"It's always best to know where you stand with your opponent, don't you think?"

"Why?" The single word was short and fervent.

"Because it's good tactics."

"I mean, why do you want to marry me?" she retorted impatiently.

"I told you last night that I wanted you," he reminded her calmly.

"Men don't marry for that reason alone," she scoffed, aware of the thrill that shot down her backbone at the searing look he gave her.

"I tried to tell you the rest of the reason last night at dinner. You didn't believe me," he murmured.

"Love at first sight?" she repeated, astounded that he should even attempt such a silly lie.

"Ummm," he agreed placidly, apparently unconcerned over whether or not she believed him.

"You think you *love* me?" she exclaimed. She felt as if he'd just rushed her guard and had landed another scoring hit. He was lying, of course, but why?

"Yes," he said frankly. "And I think I can make you love me!"

"You're basing that egotistical assumption on the way I agreed to let you kiss me?" she flung back loftily, unaware of the increased silver in her eyes.

"Like I told you, we have to start somewhere. You want me and I'm willing to take the risk that I can make you love me."

"If you did happen to be telling me the truth about your own feelings, then I should think you'd be afraid I'll confuse desire with love. Always assuming my desire for you is as overwhelming as you seem to think!"

He grinned suddenly, unexpectedly, and Kelly unconsciously fell back a step before the predatory male laughter in him. "You can't hide that female challenge in those lovely eyes. A woman only looks at a man like that when she's daring him to take her."

"Of all the egocentric, stupid, masculine reasoning!" she gasped, stunned by his audacity. "You really are a pompous example of the breed, aren't you?"

"I think," he stated slowly, the laughter dying out of his eyes as he surveyed her outraged figure, "that the rest of this conversation would be better conducted after we've both had a shower. Why don't you move that very lovely little tail of yours up that staircase before I decide to teach you how to scrub my back."

She continued to stare at him for another few very tense seconds and then she broke the spell that he was weaving with his eyes and forced herself to walk, not run, to the staircase. It took an inordinate amount of self-control, but somehow she managed not to give her tormentor the satisfaction of having her glance back at him over her shoulder.

Sweeping into the bedroom at the top of the stairs, she slammed the door behind her, yanked off her glove, and hurled it at the cedar log wall. It bounced harmlessly down onto the red and black rug, and with a groan at her loss of temper Kelly picked it up and tossed it into the duffel bag.

What a fool she had been to think she could get away with that manipulation of the data base, she told herself beratingly as she stripped the jacket and trousers from her damp body and dropped them into the bag with the glove. How could a risk be called calculated when one didn't even begin to know how to estimate the chances involved?

She glared at her image in the mirrored wall of the large

71

bathroom, automatically ripping loose the braided coil at the back of her head. An idiot. That was what she had been. But what alternative had she really had?

Her fingers ripped through the braid until the waist-length hair hung down her back. She bundled it into a towel and stepped over to the shower. There was no sense worrying about the past, she decided with characteristic resolution as she moved under the hot spray. What was done had been done, and unless she wanted to undue what good had been accomplished, she had to keep Helen from discovering the truth. Helen would be brokenhearted if she learned her own son had been so weak. . . .

But even as she accepted the knowledge that she was stuck with the situation she had created, Kelly's churning thoughts went to the man she had left at the foot of the stairs.

He'd discovered her secret and had told her the terms for which he would sell his silence. Could she afford them? And why? Why was he so determined to marry her?

She didn't believe for one moment that he had fallen in love with her. Even if he had, the knowledge of her un-scrupulous maneuvers with the computer should have been enough to kill such a delicate thing as four-day-old love!

But he hadn't seemed greatly concerned with the possibility of her being an embezzler, she thought wretchedly, turning off the water and reaching blindly around the corner of the shower stall for one of the huge chocolate-brown towels.

There had been no genuine implication that he felt torn about his duty to report her to Helen. Kelly bit her lip, considering that carefully as she toweled dry and un-wrapped her hair. In the steamy mirror she regarded her ghostly nude image, hair streaming down her back, and wondered what sort of man didn't blink an eyelid about discovering that the woman he wanted was potentially larcenous in character.

Because he thought he could control her illegal bent? Or because his own scruples weren't particularly strong in the first place?

That last wasn't a cheerful thought. An honest Locke Channing was dangerous enough. A dishonest one didn't bear contemplation!

She glanced around the long counter that housed the twin washbasins, absently noting the neat array of masculine toiletries. Locke might have been casual in his attire, but his house was surprisingly orderly. For an instant Kelly wondered what it would be like to have her own things sitting beside his on that counter.

Abruptly she turned away, the brown towel wrapped around her body and knotted at the breast. She would have to start marshaling her thoughts for the coming encounter. If Locke Channing was serious about marriage, for whatever reason, she was going to have a rough time talking him out of it. He knew he had a solid threat to use against her.

Her forehead knitted in a frown of concentration, Kelly opened the bathroom door and started into the bedroom, glancing toward the quilt where her jeans and blue velour top lay waiting. The lacy underwear was stacked on top of the velour and she reached for it automatically.

The scrap of a bra was in her hand and her fingers had gone to the knot of the towel when he moved and she saw him standing quietly beside the door.

"Locke!"

The sight of him waiting in the shadowy area to one side of the room was enough to bring out his name in a voice that almost squeaked with startled anxiety.

"I came for your answer, Kelly."

The words were unequivocal, their tone telling her he would accept only one response.

She stared at him, her stunned mind absorbing the implications of the fact that he was wearing only a pair of tight-fitting jeans. His chest was bare and he hadn't bothered to put on any shoes. The gun-black hair was still damp from the shower. He looked like the dark warlock he was, and Kelly shivered.

"What do you think you're doing here?" she managed, trying desperately for some bold parry of this new menace. "Get out."

He moved, stepping away from the wall where he had been leaning, and walking toward her with an inexorable, pacing stride.

"It occurs to me that you won't give up until you know for certain that you're beaten," he observed, all silk and metal. The jade eyes gleamed at her as he approached. The power in him seemed to wash over her in waves that lapped the air around her.

"You said we would finish the discussion later," she reminded him, hating herself for wanting to retreat in the face of his advance. She tried valiantly to inject the haughty, aloof note that might make him think she was still in control.

"This is later. I want my answer, Kelly," he grated, closing the distance as she began to step backward. "Are you going to marry me?"

"Let me get dressed," she countered cuttingly. "You've already shaken me up enough for one evening. I'll meet you downstairs in a few minutes. . . ."

The hardness in his face was immutable. She was violently, unwillingly, aware of the sleek bronzed expanse of chest and shoulders. Rough, curling hair twisted in a primitive pattern past the masculine nipples and down to the flat, hard stomach.

"I know I've given you a jolt," he agreed. "And I also know enough to realize I'd better take advantage of having got you somewhat off balance. Given enough time, you'll

74

come up with your own solution to the situation. And I can't allow that."

"Stop stalking me, dammit!"

"Stop trying to retreat," he suggested mildly, his gaze taking in the picture she made with her long hair flowing down to her waist, her modesty protected only by the towel.

She had been right the previous evening, Kelly thought. Resistance was only going to goad him further.

Her hand up to ward him off, she eyed him furiously. "Leave me alone, Locke. I won't allow you to intimidate me like this!"

"I'm not leaving this room until I have my answer."

He was almost on her now. Kelly was almost to the wall, in more ways than one.

"If you think you can force a decision like this . . ." she began, eyes brilliant and blue.

"Aren't you finding my assistance helpful?" he taunted, reaching to wrap a hand around the nape of her neck as she found the wall with her back. "Answer me, Kelly! Are you going to marry me or shall I go to Helen with the news of what you've done?"

"I've told you, I'll resign—"

"I don't want your resignation! And if I go back through that data base with a fine-tooth comb, you can bet I'll find out exactly *why* you felt obliged to make all those phony 'corrections'!"

Her eyes widened at that. She had thought his discovery of the manipulation was as far as it would go. If he learned the reason. . . .

"All right!" she gritted between clenched teeth. "I'll marry you if that's what you want. But so help me— What are you doing?"

The last was said on a shriek as he moved, hauling her forward and scooping her up into his arms.

"Taking out insurance," he told her ruthlessly as he

tossed her down into the center of the bed. "Insurance that you'll keep your word!"

An instant later he was beside her on the quilt, reaching to anchor her body with his superior strength.

CHAPTER FIVE

"Don't you dare!" Kelly bit out in savage denial, far more angry than frightened. "Take your hands off me, you arrogant fool!"

"When it comes to arrogance," he growled, throwing his blue-jeaned thigh across her bare legs, "you take the prize, sweetheart! But it's okay. Better for a woman to have too much spirit than too little."

"Why, you . . . !"

"After all," he explained, capturing a wrist in each hand and pinning them to the quilt beside her tousled head, "a man can always find ways to control the spirit, but the passion itself has to come from within."

"Passion! I'm not feeling *passionate* toward you, dammit! I'm madder than hell!"

"Only because tonight's your night to lose," he soothed, bending his head to take her lips with a quick, fierce kiss that held nothing of a soothing nature.

"If you don't stop this minute, I'm going to cry rape again," she breathed, her breasts lifting under the brown towel with the force of her panting struggles. "You said last night you'd never force yourself on me!"

A slow, anticipatory smile curved his mouth and the warlock eyes flared with rising passion as he looked down into her defiant face.

"Don't worry, my love," he whispered in a thickening voice, "I learned my lesson last night about the usefulness of honey in catching little flies with red and gold in their wings. . . ."

He touched his lips to the mass of soft brown stuff that lay in tangled tendrils across her naked shoulders, and Kelly caught her breath as the nearness of him brought his scent into her nostrils. Clean, male, and primitively inviting, it threatened to cloud her senses for an instant.

Grimly she fought free of the effect, her silvery eyes opening wide in quelling accusation as he lifted his head again to study her.

"How can you talk about loving me when you treat me like this?"

"How could I treat you like this if I didn't love you?" he countered silkily.

"Don't tease me on top of everything else," she ordered in a kind of passionate anger. "No man who loved or respected a woman would threaten her with this kind of violence."

"What kind would he threaten her with?"

"Damn you!" she hissed, frustrated beyond reason at the aggressive laughter that mingled with the passion in his eyes. "I swear I'll hate you forever—"

"No," he interrupted, the masculine humor fading at once. "You won't hate me. At least not forever."

He moved, trapping one of her arms beneath the weight of his body and holding her other wrist above her head. His free hand went to the knot of her towel but he made no immediate effort to undue it. He buried his mouth in her throat and a slow, deceptively lazy trail of kisses began to work their way up toward her lips.

"Locke, please!"

She felt the strong, sensitive fingers rest lightly on her breast as if he liked the curving shape of her beneath the towel. Against her naked thigh the roughness of his denim-covered leg seemed like the scrape of a cat's tongue on her agitated senses. And the skin of her throat was violently aware of the warmth and firmness of his mouth.

"Please what, darling?" he gritted gently, his tongue emerging to sample the taste of her shower-warmed skin. "Please love you? But I do. And I will. . . ."

"You can't!" she cried brokenly, torn between sheer fury and the growing realization that outright battle with him wasn't the way to handle the situation. Locke thrived on outright battle. "If you loved me, you wouldn't do this!"

"What would I do? Beg for your love in return? I don't think so. At least not at this stage. Do you think I want to end up with that hopeless, wistful look in my eyes that Brett Forrester has every time he watches you walk down the hall?"

"What? Locke, what the devil are you talking about?" Kelly turned her head aside from his advancing kisses, shaken by his words. It seemed she was fated to receive one shock after another tonight from this man.

"Don't pretend he doesn't want you. I've seen the expression on his face and I've heard the gossip in the computer room. But he didn't know how to go about getting you, did he? And now it's much too late, anyway. You're mine."

"You're not making any sense! Let me go and we can—can talk things over at dinner." Gamely Kelly sought for a reasonable alternative to offer him.

"Dinner can wait." He began untying the knot of the towel, ignoring her startled gasp. "Right now it's more important to consolidate my victory."

"Victory!" she yelped, twisting violently in one last evasion attempt that proved fruitless. "That's all this has been for you tonight, hasn't it?"

"It's definitely been a part of the evening's festivities," he agreed on a note of deepening intent and wonder as he unwrapped the towel to expose her small firm breasts.

79

"My God, but I want you!" He seemed a little dazed by his own kindling need, Kelly thought blankly, not understanding the longing in his eyes. She shivered as he palmed one breast, knowing even as she fought to control it that the traitorous nipple was being coaxed out of hiding.

"Locke, no! You promised you wouldn't—"

"Hush, Kelly. There will be no rape," he told her steadily, raising suddenly serious eyes to meet hers. "Kiss me," he commanded softly. "Kiss me like you did last night and I give you my word I won't force you."

She stared up at him, trying to read the meaning in his words and his expression.

"You swear you won't?" she got out on a panting whisper.

"I love you, Kelly," he broke in, the yearning in him very plain now. "And you're going to marry me. Kiss me and give me some of your warmth tonight. It will be like last night."

"Another forfeit?" she hedged uncertainly, not fully trusting him.

"If you want to call it that. After all, you did lose tonight."

"Because of your damn psychological warfare!"

"A man uses the weapons that come to hand," he murmured absently, his lips feathering the line of her brow and then the tip of her nose.

"Kiss me," he repeated, his mouth hovering a bare inch above hers.

"Do you love me, Locke?" she asked in curious wonder.

"Yes."

The single word was crisp, unequivocal, absolutely certain.

"I don't understand . . ." she began helplessly, trying to sort through the possibilities of the situation. If he truly did love her, or even if he was only fascinated by her as he had claimed, he was vulnerable. But vulnerable men

always wanted something from her. Something other than
~~love. What did Locke Channing want from her?~~ How did
he mean to use her?

"Take my word for it," he advised dryly. "It happens.
You'll see."

Kelly waited no longer. She would give him his kiss, just
as she had last night. His declaration of love confused her,
but it also served to make the command virtually irresistible.

She touched her lips with the tip of her tongue and
parted them with instinctive invitation. With a groan he
lowered his mouth and took the offering.

She sensed the way he reveled in the caress, felt the need
in him as it tautened his muscles. The leg he had thrown
across her thighs tightened, but Kelly realized vaguely it
was an unconscious reaction on his part. He was no longer
deliberately trying to trap her.

His mouth moved slowly, lingeringly on hers, urging
admittance for his questing tongue. She gave it, knowing
it was too soon to protest. As she had last night, she would
have to give enough to satisfy his immediate demands. In
a few minutes she would put up the barriers. . . .

He searched her mouth with a hungering need, his
tongue finding hers in a passionate little duel that reminded her for some strange reason of the one they had just
fought downstairs. His fingers found the pulse at the base
of her neck and wandered slowly, languidly, back down to
the thrusting tips of her breasts.

"I want you so much," he husked, dragging his mouth
away from hers to search out the delicate area behind her
ear.

For some crazy reason it all seemed to be flowing
together, Kelly acknowledged vaguely, twisting one hand
free to find the thickness of his black hair with her fingers.
First the victory in armed combat combined with the
intellectual master stroke of telling her he knew about her

81

manipulation of the computer. Added to that was his immediate insistence on marriage and then the demand for her agreement. Now this slow, building arousal of her senses.

There was a distinct danger in the pattern, but Kelly was finding it harder and harder to keep her mind on it. She was discovering that she loved the feel of the damp gun-metal-colored hair, and just below that were the sleek, strong muscles of his neck and shoulders. Their resiliency seemed to appeal to her fingers in an uncanny fashion.

Soon, she promised herself, arching her neck in response to his kiss, she would call a halt and claim she had given him his forfeit. A shiver coursed through her as he used his teeth with gentle menace on the skin of her shoulder. Her toes curled tightly in response and one knee lifted unconsciously. The undone towel parted completely.

Instantly his hand stroked down from breast to stomach to thigh. He found the inside of the raised knee and began tracing tiny circles upward toward the center of her warmth.

"Locke?"

His name was a questioning, uncertain little sound. "Not so fast, please," Kelly heard herself beg. "I need time. I'm not sure how much I want—"

"We'll find out how much you want," he vowed hoarsely, his lips moving down the curve of her breast to find the nipple.

"Oh . . ." The almost-agony was exquisite. With a sudden, convulsive grip Kelly clutched him to her, her hands sliding along the muscles of his back and down to the lean waist.

"That's right, my little adversary," he breathed tightly, trembling in response to her grasp. "Touch me, hold me, want me . . ."

His fingers on her thigh were prowling closer to his ultimate goal, and Kelly made a shaking effort to deny him further intimacy. But when she tried to press her legs together, he somehow slid his jeaned thigh between them. To her now racing senses, the action signaled yet another defeat.

"No!" The protest was weak, even to her own ears, and Locke paid it no heed.

"I only want to love you, sweetheart. I need so badly to make you mine. Can't you give me that much?" Each word was a tangle of masculine command and pleading, punctuated by tiny nibbling kisses that forged a way between her breasts and toward the opposite nipple.

"Locke, I don't want—" She licked her lips, eyes squeezed shut against the overwhelming sensations assaulting her body. "I can't let you—"

Then, quite suddenly, his hand had found the unbearably sensitive, intimate warmth it had been stalking and his teeth closed simultaneously on the tip of one breast.

Kelly moaned with unleashed desire. Abandoning her last efforts at rational thought and control, she turned into his heat with a driving urge to consummate the final victory. Fumbling with passion, her fingers slid along the inside waistband of his jeans and found the snap and zipper.

He groaned in heavy passion, arching his narrow hips as she fought to undress him. In another frenzied moment he lay naked beside her, his need a blatant power his body could not hide.

She touched the rough thigh with a hunger she didn't have time to analyze. It was overpowering, urgent, dominant. She could only give herself up to the astonishing excitement of the moment.

Locke stroked her whole body with his hands and his lips, rolling onto his back and pulling her in a passionate sprawl across his chest. His fingers sank into the softness of her buttocks, impelling her closer and closer to his own hardness.

"You want me," he muttered fiercely, using his short nails on her smooth skin. "Tell me you want me."

"I want you," Kelly repeated obediently, willing to give him anything he asked in that moment of unreal passion. "I've never wanted anyone like this. I didn't realize . . ."

The words trailed off. She couldn't complete the sentence, partly because she couldn't think coherently enough to formulate her thoughts and partly because her mouth was too busy dropping hot, wet little kisses on first the skin of his stomach and then on the flat nipples.

Her hands moved in swift, butterfly touches, which brought deep, hungry sounds from Locke's throat. Each response she drew from him now seemed to inflame her further.

When her hair swirled across his chest and hips, he shifted abruptly, grasping a huge handful of it and using it with gentle ruthlessness to force her onto her back.

"I can't wait any longer, sweetheart," he grated, his strong, lean body covering hers with a mastery she couldn't have fought even if she still wanted to do so.

Kelly was chaotically aware of a swirling variety of impressions, including the roughness of masculine thighs as he parted her legs, the unbreakable grip of his hands on her shoulders, and the sheer forceful weight of his body as he came down on her in a controlled passion that inflamed her own.

"Oh, Locke! Locke!"

His name was a gasp, half blocked in her throat as he completed the union with the power and grace of a fencer's lunge. Her body lifted to meet his with instinctive response, a dazzling parry and riposte, which only served to incite his need of her.

She sensed that need in all its naked strength and dominion. Every nerve and trained muscle in her body sought to satisfy it and, in so doing, satisfy itself.

The explosion of desire seemed to mushroom around her, filling the room and her body. She was aware of his taut shoulders beneath her nails, heard his harsh exclamation of desire, and then his fingers were at work on her hips.

The cadence of the sensuous fencing match absorbed all Kelly's senses. She responded recklessly to the demands of Locke's lovemaking, issuing equally bold demands of her own.

He had no hesitation about meeting them. The wild, primitive attack, parry, counter-parry, beat, and lunge caught them both in the fascination of the duel.

"Kelly, my own, my love!"

His cry came as he felt her go suddenly rigid and then dissolve into a violent uncontrolled shiver beneath him.

"Oh, my God! My God!" she breathed over and over again as the force of the culmination shook her. Never had she known such power, such oneness with an adversary.

Before her body could find its equilibrium, she felt Locke's own mindless release as his body arced with primitive male strength. She held him tightly as he clung to her, each drawing the last vestige of passion from the other.

It seemed forever before her breathing returned to its normal rhythm. Kelly lay wrapped in a tangle of arms and legs, dimly aware that the sheen of dampness on her skin was as great as it had been when she'd finished the duel downstairs.

Her head against his hard chest, she listened vaguely to the sounds that told her that Locke, too, was recovering from the lovemaking. Eyes wide and almost stunned, she stared at the soft rise and fall of stomach and tried to think logically about how to handle the next few minutes.

Dazedly she tried to understand what had happened. But the only clear, diamond-hard thought that formed in her mind was that she had given him everything tonight.

Her defeat had been total, carried out on too many levels to allow for any last-minute foxholes in which to hide.

All of which led to the one overriding question left between them. When she felt his hand move with idle gentleness in her hair, she asked it.

"What do you want from me, Locke?"

The hand in her hair paused for a moment and then she felt, rather than saw, his smile above her head.

"Want from you?" he repeated lazily. "That's simple enough to answer. I want all of you. I want you here in my bed at night. I want to have you as my permanent fencing opponent. I want to know you won't look at any other man. I want to share a glass of wine with you before dinner in the evenings. I want—"

"Stop it!" she pleaded bitterly, twisting back to face him. His hand fell away from her hair as silver-blue eyes clashed violently with the jade-green gaze. "You don't have to go through all that nonsense. Just tell me what you want!"

He stared at her intense expression, his eyes lingering on the slightly bruised lips. He lifted a finger to touch them and smiled caressingly.

"I want you. I don't know how much simpler a man can get with words."

She stared at him, trying to decipher the hidden meanings that must be there. "I'm not a fool, Locke, even though after tonight you probably think I am."

With his finger he pressed down on her lower lip in a small surprisingly sensuous caress. Deliberately she pulled her head back, away from his touch. The warlock eyes lifted to hers.

"What are you expecting me to say?" he finally asked.

She lifted one shoulder in an attempt at a negligent gesture. "I'm trying to save us both some time."

He considered that. "The only other thing I could add to the list"—she tensed and Locke frowned, clearly not understanding her reaction—"is a wish to have you love me too."

"Locke, please! You've won everything tonight. Can't you at least be honest in return?"

The line of his mouth tightened and he slowly levered himself up to a sitting position against the pillows. Very deliberately he pulled her up beside him, holding her firmly against his length.

"I think we'd better take this from the top," he announced determinedly, his hand around her waist under the flow of hair. "I'm not sure what you thought I was doing tonight, but I'll try and make my position quite plain."

"Don't be condescending," she muttered without thinking.

"Hey!" he rebuked, half-joking, "is that any way to talk to the man who just made passionate love to you? The man you're going to marry?"

"And don't try cajoling me either!"

"Watch your tongue, vixen, or I won't bother with any more conversation. When you lash me with that sarcasm of yours, it's always a temptation to shut you up with a kiss. And now that I know exactly how well you respond to my lovemaking, I can guarantee I won't stop with only a kiss!"

Kelly gritted her teeth but said nothing, willing him to go on with his explanation. She had to know the worst.

"Now, then," he muttered quite equably as he sensed her silent submission. "I've told you everything I want from you. I want you to love me. Passionately, irrevocably, and completely. There, I've answered your question. Tell me why you asked it."

Kelly turned slightly in his hold, once again meeting his eyes with a searching silver-blue gaze. "Are you going to sit there and tell me you don't want anything besides *me?*"

"Guilty as charged," he grinned.

"You don't want my help in getting you more work at Forrester Stereo?" she dared, eyes narrowing.

"Honey, I've got more work than I can handle already. I don't need any more contracts with Forrester Stereo for the rest of my life!" he exploded impatiently.

"You didn't seem particularly concerned with the ethics of my association with the computer," she went on determinedly. "Does that mean you've been up to a few tricks yourself? Tricks you're afraid I'll discover and tell Helen about once you've gone?"

"You crazy little idiot! If I wanted to pull off a computer caper with Forrester's machine, I'd fix it so neither you nor anyone else would find out about it until it was much too late to stop me!"

"All right, that lets out business reasons, providing you're telling me the truth." She ignored his arrogantly lifted dark brow and plunged on. "That leaves personal matters."

"It sure does."

"I know about your ex-fiancée. Are you planning on asking me to act as some sort of shield against her? Do you still love her? Or have you been working on some stupid plan of revenge? Are you going to use me in some way against her?"

"I don't know whether to laugh at you or beat you!" he growled in open astonishment. "What the hell is this inquisition all about?"

"Just answer the questions!" she blazed.

"The answer is no! To all of them! I don't know how you found out about Amanda, but she's out of my life and has been for several months. We bored each other to tears, for God's sake! You don't sit around and plot revenge against a woman who nearly put you to sleep with her constant chatter about clothes and filmstars!"

Kelly blinked owlishly. "Is there any other woman in your life? An ex-wife? Or a current one for that matter?"

"No!"

"Then what the hell do you want from me?" Kelly wailed in frustration.

"I'm beginning to think some sort of reasonable explanation might be in order," he answered savagely. "It's your turn. Tell me what this is all about before I strangle you! Has every man you've ever known wanted something from you? Something along the lines of the things you just mentioned?"

"Yes!"

Kelly closed her mouth at once, appalled at the heedless way in which she'd given him her answer. She tried to lean away from him, acutely aware of her nudity as well as his.

"Ah!" he breathed on a long sigh. "I'm beginning to understand. Forget that," he added brusquely as she scrabbled to pull the edge of the quilt across her thighs. "I like you the way you are. Now look at me and tell me if I've got this straight at last."

"Locke, I don't want to talk about this anymore. . . ."

"You started this conversation, by God, you're going to finish it."

She lowered her eyes sullenly, only to have her chin jerked up a second later.

"You're a strong woman, Kelly Winfield. A strong mind, a strong body, and strong passions. I saw all that the first time I looked at you, and a lot of other men have probably been equally perceptive. Good Lord! It doesn't take much to see you're a survivor in this world. You wear the aura like a cloak. I can well believe men have latched onto you, instinctively wanting to make use of your power. Power is a tremendously attractive quality in a human being. It's a survival trait and all of us automatically respond to it. You, apparently, ran into a few men who realized they were onto a useful thing. What happened, sweetheart? Did you fall in love with them before you realized they weren't capable of loving you with the same degree of passion?"

"Locke, I've told you I don't want to discuss it!"

"Well, we're going to discuss it and that's that. Am I right so far in my analysis?" He gave her a small shake when she didn't immediately answer.

"More or less. But I didn't make the mistake of falling in love with them!"

"I thought so," he nodded. "But they probably thought themselves in love with you often enough. And when they asked you to help them out of some mess they'd got themselves into, you felt sorry for them and did what you could, right?"

"Past tense," she hissed. "I don't make that error anymore."

"Except with me. I make love to you and before I've even caught my breath afterward, you're demanding to know what I want from you. Why, Kelly? Because for me you were prepared to make that error again?"

"No!" she flung back wretchedly.

"Liar," he teased affectionately. "I think you were ready to give me anything I wanted. You're committed to me now, sweetheart. I don't think you even realize the depths of your own surrender tonight."

"One evening in your bed doesn't indicate a grand surrender, you arrogant, complacent, self-satisfied man!"

"*This* evening does," he whispered throatily, smiling into her stormy eyes. "I told you earlier this was your night to lose. At everything. I beat you at fencing, I beat you at your little game with the computer, and I made you respond to me with all the passion that's in you—and that's a considerable amount, I'm pleased to say. I realized last night that you were going to have to lose and lose big to a man before you could acknowledge him as your equal. So I hit you with the whole arsenal tonight."

"How can you sit there and brag like that?" Kelly whispered, shocked at his relentless words.

"I'm not bragging, honey," he soothed. "I'm explaining how you wound up in my bed tonight. But you still don't understand, do you?"

"I understand that you caught me in a weak moment and I got carried away by perfectly human emotions. . . ."

"No." He brushed her protest aside with an impatient flick of his hand, green eyes hardening intently. "I mean you don't understand the real reason you wanted to know what I was going to ask of you."

"I'm sure you'll enlighten me," she snapped, goaded.

"My pleasure. You wanted to know what the price was for my love because you were prepared to pay it. And you were prepared to pay it because you're falling in love with me, not because you're feeling sorry for me."

Kelly went very still. "That's not true," she finally said on a thin thread of sound. It couldn't be true!

"You mean you're prepared to pay it because you *do* feel sorry for me?" he mocked lightly.

"Stop twisting my words!"

"You don't feel sorry for me, do you?" he retorted complacently.

"Of course I don't! How could any woman feel sorry for such a pompous, egotistical male!"

"Who just beat you hands down at everything that counts," he concluded helpfully.

"How," she demanded with regal grace, "could I possibly love a man who gloated so in his little victories?"

"You can love him because he's proved himself as strong as you are, because you need him as much as he needs you, and because you don't have to feel sorry for him. I shall ask a great deal of you in the future, Kelly Winfield, but not one fraction more than I'm willing to give in return. And that equality in the giving and receiving is what makes everything different for us."

"What makes you the authority?" she muttered, feeling the pull of the metal and silk words on her senses and not understanding how to fight it.

He smiled ruefully. "I haven't existed in a vacuum for the past thirty-five years. I've learned a few lessons along the way too."

"Lessons from people like Amanda Bailey?"

"It takes all kinds of teachers," he retorted philosophically.

"Did she fascinate you at first too? When did the boredom set in, Locke? After you'd slept with her or when she refused to sleep with you? Did you try your comprehensive siege tactics against her? Did they fail?"

He stopped her tirade with a hard, punishing kiss that sapped her breath. Nor did he lift his head until she'd tacitly abandoned the field.

"Forget Amanda. Forget everyone else. We're going to be married, Kelly. You and I are the only ones who count now. I love you and I've made you mine. Whether you like it or not, you're committed to me and I think you know it, deep down inside. Stop fighting, Kelly. The war is over."

Over! she thought near-hysterically, staring up at him as if he were some pagan male from another planet who had come to carry her off. Their war wasn't over. It had only begun! Didn't he realize that?

Did he expect her to have become blind and stupid in defeat? Did he really believe she was going to fall for his lies of love? She would make him admit the real reason he wanted to marry her if it was the last thing she accomplished on earth!

Men didn't fall in love with her, they used her strength and then wondered why she lost interest in them. Locke

Channing might be cleverer than the others, but she would unmask him all the same.

"I can see you're not very gracious in defeat," he chuckled, leaning over to drop a kiss on her forehead. "But I'm not prepared to continue this conversation on an empty stomach. Back to the showers, my love, and then downstairs to the steaks!"

"Steaks," she muttered, appalled. "How can you think of food at a time like this?"

He swung his legs to the floor, rising tall and uncompromisingly male beside the bed. Hands on hips, he grinned devilishly down at her.

"A time like this is when I think about food the most! A little personality quirk for you to store in that able memory of yours, honey. Sex makes me hungry. Some men need a cigarette afterward; I need food!"

"That doesn't strike you as a little unromantic?" she quipped, sliding off the opposite edge of the bed and reaching quickly for the chocolate towel.

"Shame on you! Aren't you going to find it terribly romantic to cook your first meal for me?"

He was already at the bedroom door and through it, blue jeans in one hand, when the chocolate towel hurtled after him. The tightly wadded material harmlessly struck the spot where he would have been if Kelly had been a fraction faster. The accuracy didn't surprise her. She took the fencing-induced eye-hand coordination for granted. What bothered her was that he had been too fast for her.

CHAPTER SIX

In the end Locke had broiled the steaks, a vigilant eye on the expensive meat while he cheerfully gave orders concerning the salad and wine. He hadn't seemed to notice the silent, unenthusiastic manner in which Kelly carried out the directions. Nor did he pay any attention to the speculative, assessing glances she tossed at him from time to time.

But he hadn't argued after dinner when she'd quietly asked to be taken home. He'd looked up suddenly from the last of his zinfandel wine, and she'd been certain he was going to protest. But he refrained, although there was no doubting the taut quality of his aggressive jawline.

Deliberately he'd set down the glass and smiled across the round hardwood table. "It's a temptation to tell you you're not going to spend the night anywhere else except in my bed, but," he'd added quickly, catching the bluing silver of her eyes, "I think maybe I've pushed you enough this evening. You look exhausted, my love, and I don't want you appearing worn and wan at work tomorrow. People might find it hard to believe the happy bride bit!"

"I can understand that. I don't believe it myself!"

"Good. You're reviving," he chuckled approvingly. "Finally get it all sorted out in that sharp little mind?"

"There are a few loose ends," she acknowledged tightly.

But those were cleared up when he walked her to the apartment door sometime later. He pulled her into his arms with surprising gentleness, his mouth warm and persuasive on hers.

"It's all right, sweetheart," he murmured after a moment, his lips moving in her hair near her ear. "You can tell me. I'll take care of everything."

Kelly stiffened, warning bells chiming loudly in her bemused brain.

"Tell you what?" Her hands were wedged against his chest in silent protest, although he must have sensed the way her lips had responded to his.

"Why you did it, of course," he said with a lightness that didn't deceive her. This was no joke. Locke wanted an answer.

"Locke, what are you talking about?" But she knew. Finally it was all becoming clear.

"Fiddle with the financial data in the Forrester computer," he said mildly, as if he were asking for nothing more than the solution to a puzzle that had thus far defeated him.

"I thought," Kelly said very carefully, tilting her head back to meet the jade eyes, "that with your virtuoso abilities on the computer you could figure that out for yourself!"

"It would take time," he admitted ruefully. "And the answers might not be conclusive. I'd much rather you told me yourself."

Kelly sucked in her breath, eyes flashing up at him. "I think not. You've had more than your share of wins tonight. I wouldn't want to make it all too easy for you. You might lose interest!"

She whirled out of his arms, twisted her key in the lock, and stepped into the safety of her own apartment. Turning, she slammed the door very calmly and deliberately in his face.

And then she slid the deadbolt into place as an added precaution.

Damn the man! So that's what it had all been about! Kelly swept through the sophisticated brass-, glass-, and leather-furnished living room, strange, frustrated rage growing in her.

She would never have dreamed a man would go so far to solve a puzzle! But what did it all mean? How much did Locke know, and more importantly, how much did Helen know?

Kelly shook her head in gathering dismay as she considered the consequences. With a violent tug she pulled off the blue velour top and stalked into the bedroom with its brass bed to finish undressing.

Desperately she tried to think logically. Pulling on a Chinese-red robe, she turned out the light and walked over to the window, gazing out at the twinkling lights on the lake's shore.

There was only one logical sequence of events that explained the whole mess. Locke must have discovered the manipulation of the data base early in his investigation of the inventory problem. He'd gone straight to Helen with his suspicions. Helen, after being told that one of her most trusted managers was the suspect, had quietly told Locke to find out why the data had been "corrected."

And Locke, with a directness Kelly decided was probably typical of him, simply sought the easiest path to the answers. He would seduce the culprit and coax the explanation out of her.

Kelly's small fist struck the window frame in self-disgust and pain, both physical and mental. Well, she had her answer. She now knew what Locke wanted from her. To give the devil his due, he was asking for something altogether different from any of the other men in her life had asked. The others had wanted her strength. Locke wanted to defeat her. Totally.

He had come very close tonight, she thought bitterly, turning away from the window and heading toward the bed with its ivory quilt. His strategy had been brilliant. Who could have guessed that she would have surrendered so completely to the one man who had demonstrated his strength to her instead of his weakness?

Or perhaps it stood to reason, she decided miserably as she slipped off the robe and climbed into bed. Perhaps it was inevitable that after so many years of finding herself in the role of comforter, sympathetic ear, and female tower of strength she would succumb to the one man who pitted his strength against hers.

She had been a fool tonight, but now she knew the full truth. The question of what to do next remained, however. Worrying about it kept her awake for hours. That, in itself, was significant, she thought grimly. Kelly seldom worried about a problem. She simply set about solving it.

She was still worrying about it, however, at nine o'clock the next morning as she sat at her desk and sipped a cup of tea. Of all the possible solutions the only one that seemed practical was to go to Helen and hand in her resignation. The difficulty there lay in the fact that the role of martyr didn't come easily.

Which left the option of confronting Brett. Kelly's fingers drummed idly on the desk while she considered that. What would Brett do? It had been several months since the incident. How did he feel about it now?

The door opened as she was in the process of running through a variety of mental arguments, including the possibility that Locke had been bluffing when he said he could get the information he needed from the computer.

"Good morning, sweetheart," Locke greeted her, standing in the doorway with a huge pile of computer printouts stacked in his arms. She met his green gaze over the top of the stack and said nothing, waiting.

"You'll be pleased to learn that I have just commandeered that desk over there by the window," he went on blithely, heading for the long worktable Kelly used for certain projects. He dumped the computer printouts down onto the desk and turned back to face her with a perceptive smile.

He was wearing his usual corduroy jacket over the casually unbuttoned shirt, and his thick black hair looked slightly windblown. He'd probably combed it before leaving home that morning but hadn't bothered to repeat the process after arriving at work. The new storm front approaching from the ocean had brought brisk winds.

"Why?" Kelly sipped her tea and watched him the way a rabbit watches a cobra.

"Because I have now come to the part of the business I hate most: writing the final report for management. And I couldn't concentrate down in the computer room with all the racket from the printer and the constant chatter. Besides, this will give us a chance to get to know each other a little better, don't you think?"

He folded his arms and leaned back against the desk, one brow cocked wryly as she simply continued to sit and watch him.

"I notice you're not running into my arms for a good-morning kiss," he observed.

"I don't seem to feel terribly energetic this morning."

"Ah, brooding over last night, are we?"

"Not exactly. I'm doing some of the thinking I should have done last night." Kelly informed him coldly, her narrowed eyes never leaving his harshly carved face. She could see the memory of the previous night in his warm, green gaze and wanted to slap the tanned cheek.

"Thinking wouldn't have done you any good last night, honey," he assured her sympathetically. "I was a step ahead of you all evening."

"Only a step?"

"That's all it takes. A small edge decides the outcome of a battle," he grinned unrepentantly. He straightened

98

and walked over to where she sat, then reached down to lift the cup out of her hand and haul her up beside him.

"But now the war is over, my love," he whispered deeply. "And you were most generous in your surrender. . . ."

Kelly's hand had curled into a fist with which she might very well have hit him if the door hadn't suddenly been flung open.

"Kelly! I just heard the news. What's all this about—Oh!"

Brett's stunned eyes took in the sight of Locke's arms wrapped around her, and for an instant the three of them simply stared at each other.

"Hello, Brett," Kelly said as calmly as possible, pulling herself free and taking her seat. She was aware that Locke was coolly making himself at home, sliding familiarly onto the edge of her desk. The toe of one large leather shoe swung negligently as he looked across the room toward Brett.

"I see you've heard about our engagement," Locke said smoothly. "Come to congratulate us?"

"Helen told me," the younger man said quietly, his eyes on Kelly's composed face. "I expect she'll be along in a minute to give you her best, Kelly."

"I didn't know you'd made a general announcement, Locke," Kelly said with a touch of accusation.

He glanced down at her and smiled one of those smiles that didn't reach his eyes. She knew he was reacting to Brett's presence the way a successful lion would react to a smaller cat who threatened to steal the hunt's takings.

"I mentioned it to her when I arrived a few minutes ago. Apparently she didn't waste any time in telling Brett."

"It'll be all over the office in a few minutes," Brett agreed laconically. "Her secretary, Carol, heard her tell me."

99

Kelly shrugged noncommittally, aware of the tension in Locke.

"Have you set a date?" Brett asked with rather formal politeness.

Kelly smiled grimly and glanced pointedly at Locke. Let him get himself out of that query.

He caught her look but turned his attention to Brett. "No, but it will be soon. Neither of us wants to wait."

Kelly's eyes silvered at the lie and she reached for the remains of her tea with fingers that trembled. Of course there would be no date set. Locke had no intention of marrying her, only seducing her to the point where he could get his puzzle solved. It would serve him right if she pressed for a date. . . .

"There's no need to wait more than a few days, is there, darling?" she heard herself say in a taunting drawl. Deliberately she fixed him with a longing gaze as his head snapped around. "A couple of days to get the legalities taken care of and organize the move from my apartment into your home. . . . Why, we could be married the first of next week!"

She saw the sudden wariness in him and wanted to laugh. Abruptly she felt better than she had all night.

She knew he saw the laughter in her. She made no attempt to hide it. His confusion was proof of the success of her unexpected attack. Locke Channing was being forced back to a defensive position. She waited to see how he would parry.

"You're quite right, sweetheart," he retorted coolly. "I'll—uh—have to see about getting a license. . . ."

"Shouldn't be any problem," she nodded encouragingly.

"Look, I'll leave you two to work out the details," Brett interrupted hurriedly, backing out the door. "I only came by to—er—congratulate you. We can talk later, Kelly."

She flicked a glance at the closing door as he left. Yes, they would have to talk. And the sooner the better.

"Well, you made that easy enough," Locke noted quietly, not moving from his perch on her desk. "I was prepared for all kinds of trouble from him."

"Perhaps you're not as good as you like to think you are when it comes to analyzing a tricky situation."

"Meaning?" he demanded dryly.

"You're the one who's good at solving puzzles. Work it out for yourself. Now, if you don't mind, I've got a lot to do today."

He leaned forward with pantherlike swiftness and caught her face between his two rough hands. The green eyes glittered dangerously as he studied her mutinous expression.

"Enjoy playing boss with your hired gun while you can, sweetheart. But keep in mind how much more dangerous I am than your normal run of employees!"

"More threats, Locke?"

"You know the answer to that," he retorted, sliding off the desk and heading across the room to the desk beside the window. "They're promises, of course."

In the end Helen didn't drop by Kelly's office. She sent for her shortly before noon while Kelly was immersed in a budget report. Marcie Reynolds, who had been delighted by the unexpected romance that had blossomed under her nose, gave her boss the message.

"Tell her I'll be right there, Marcie." Kelly smiled politely, her brain starting to churn again. Was it necessary for all of them to go through this charade?

She got to her feet, glancing suspiciously at Locke's dark head. He didn't even look up from the printout spread out in front of him. As soon as he'd taken his seat after Brett's departure, he'd become totally absorbed in his project. Looking at him now, Kelly could well imagine that the ex-fiancée had got fairly short shrift the day she'd handed back the ring. If the poor girl had walked in on him while he was involved with his precious programming work, it was a wonder she'd even managed to get her message across.

It was almost intriguing how passionately intent Locke became with whatever project he had set himself to, whether it be work or a fencing match—or making love. Kelly winced and made her way quickly down the hall. Allowing herself to be intrigued by Locke Channing was risky business.

"So the green eyes got you, did they?" Helen smiled kindly, perhaps a little ruefully as Kelly walked into her office. "I guess Locke really does know how to use his bait. I must admit, I didn't think he'd be angling for marriage though. I had the feeling he was distinctly relieved to be rid of poor Amanda!"

Kelly smiled, using an abnormal quota of willpower to keep her nervousness from showing. How much did Helen know? She was beginning to feel like a small animal caught in a trap while Locke and Helen slowly tightened the strings.

"I'm not sure he quite realizes what he's done," she managed truthfully, thinking of the way he had reacted when she'd told Brett the marriage could be held soon.

"You mean our computer wizard has finally met his match?"

"We'll know if he shows up for his wedding, won't we?"

Helen eyed her interestedly. "Perhaps you're the one to handle him, Kelly. But it's all happening rather quickly, isn't it? But, then, from what I know of Locke, that's reasonable."

"Oh, I don't know," Kelly murmured distantly. "He didn't rush the marriage with Amanda Bailey, did he? And we haven't set a firm date yet. Perhaps Locke likes the process of getting engaged."

Helen stared at her uncertainly. "Kelly . . . I . . ."

"Never mind, Helen. I'm only teasing you. And you're absolutely right. It is all happening rather quickly. But don't worry about me. I can look after myself."

"Yes." The older woman smiled, looking more pleased. "I know."

Kelly walked out of her boss's office a few minutes later with the invitation to the Saturday evening party Helen was giving burning a hold in her mind. Today was Friday, which meant she had another day to think. She would wait before mentioning the invitation to Locke. Dammit! *Had* Locke told Helen? Were they plotting against her? The older woman had seemed as genuinely nice as ever. . . .

"Kelly, have you got a minute?"

She glanced at Brett's good-looking face and smiled politely. "Yes, I do, and you were right this morning. We need to talk, Brett." With sudden decision she walked into his office and shut the door firmly behind her.

"For the love of God, Kelly! What's going on?" Brett's blond eyebrows were knitted together in frowning concern as he motioned her to a seat. "You hardly know the guy! How can you be talking of marriage already?"

"It's a long and somewhat confusing story," she admitted wryly, sinking into the offered chair and crossing her legs. Idly she adjusted the hem of her beige slit skirt. "It has to do with my fancy footwork on the computer a few months ago."

"Kelly!"

Her mouth quirked at his shocked look. "He knows, Brett. And I can't figure out if he's told your mother."

Brett swore softly, violently, and the pencil in his fingers snapped.

"But I don't get it. Why hasn't someone said something? I can't see Helen turning a blind eye to *that*!"

"I don't think she is. But you see, he doesn't know why I did it," she told him very smoothly, watching for his reaction. She knew what to expect, was braced for it, but for some reason she hoped that this time Brett could be stronger than his past record indicated.

He took a deep breath. "You mean he knows about you but not about me?"

"It would appear so. He wants an explanation, however."

"And so far you haven't given it?" he demanded bleakly.

"No."

"What's the marriage got to do with all this?" Brett asked wretchedly, the anxiety clear on his handsome features.

"I'm being seduced into admitting the truth."

"My God, Kelly! Are you serious?"

She shrugged. "It's the only explanation I've come up with. Locke knows about the data being manipulated and now he wants an explanation. He's pretending to have fallen in love with me. I didn't know what else to do except go along with it until I've figured out a logical way to handle the mess."

"It doesn't sound as if there is one!"

"That may be."

"I could go to Helen. . . ." The words were reluctant and low.

"It would crush her."

"Don't you think I know that?" Brett surged to his feet in restless frustration, and paced the floor in front of his window. "If only I hadn't been such a complete and total fool. How could I have been so stupid, Kelly? I'll never forgive myself—"

"It's done," she interrupted, not wanting to listen to the postmortem. The present and future were what counted now. "We've got to think of a way out."

He looked at her blankly.

"*I've* got to think of a way out," she amended sardonically, getting to her feet and starting toward the door.

"Kelly, wait. I'm not going to let you take the rap for this!"

"I don't intend to, Brett," she murmured with determination. "My willingness to help you out of a scrape stops short of martyrdom. Give me some time." She opened the door, still looking back at him over her shoulder. "I'll come up with something."

She turned back to make her exit and nearly collided with Locke, who stood, hand raised to knock on the door she had just opened.

"Locke!"

"I came to find you for lunch, Kelly," he said in a remote, metallic tone that told her he sensed the intimate tension in the room. How much had he heard?

"Fine," she managed to say quickly, not liking the way the warlock eyes were going past her face to focus on Brett. "I'll get my purse."

Lunch was the last thing she wanted at the moment, especially in Locke's company, but anything was better than standing there and waiting for all hell to break loose. Firmly she shut the door, sealing off Brett from the potential danger.

The storm broke over her head but not quite in the way she had feared. Expecting to be confronted with demands for an explanation of what she and Brett had been plotting, she was shocked when Locke turned the full force of the anger of a possessive man on her the moment they reached the black Jaguar.

"What the hell do you think you're doing slipping off to Forrester's office for a private little chat?" he grated, slamming the car into gear and heading toward the somewhat rambling downtown district. The heavy morning rainstorm had left the air clear and bright, and toward the east the snow sparkled on the Cascades. The jagged peaks

105

clawed skyward with the ruggedness of a geologically young mountain range.

"It was business," she declared stiffly, still wondering how much he had heard. Why was he taking the outraged-male approach? Why not a demand for information on the computer scheme?

"Business, my—" he began to explode, shooting her a violent look.

"Where are we going for lunch?" she broke in determinedly.

He named a popular restaurant noted for its seafood. "Kelly, listen to me and listen good. I know you're accustomed to running your past relationships—"

"What makes you say that?" she asked, startled.

"It's obvious. You were always the strong one. And besides, you told me yourself the men you've known have usually wanted something from you, something of a *practical* nature. It stands to reason they probably let you control things in the hopes they'd get what they wanted. But that's not the way it's going to be between us!"

"Why not? You want something too, don't you?" she gritted angrily.

"I'm the man in your life who wants something different. I want *you*! I'm a possessive man, Kelly. I don't have any intention of sharing you with the others. If they were too weak to hang on to you, that's their problem. I'm not going to make the same mistake."

"Are you trying to tell me you're jealous, Locke Channing?"

"As hell," he agreed immediately, profile very set and grim.

She stared at him, quite suddenly believing his words. It didn't make any sense, she told herself all through lunch and at several points during the afternoon. It just didn't make any sense. Was he deceiving her?

No, she decided shortly before closing time. Locke

Channing wasn't that good an actor. Perhaps last night had meant more to him than he'd intended it to. . . . And perhaps he hadn't yet told Helen about his discovery. . . .

She was romanticizing a very dangerous situation, Kelly thought fleetingly, aware she'd got little done during the afternoon. The incident didn't have the same effect on Locke. When they returned from a rather strained lunch, he buried himself once more in the printouts, channeling his aggressive energy into his work. But something told her he'd meant every word of the lecture he'd given her over lunch.

Jealous. The single word ricocheted around her mind like loose shrapnel. What if, in gaining his victory last night, Locke had begun to succumb to his own elaborate plot? She remembered his passionate lovemaking and saw it now from a slightly different angle. Could any man fake that degree of tender aggression unless he felt something for the woman he held in his arms?

The thought sent a small unbelievable thrill along her nerves. When Locke finally tossed down his pencil, shut the computer printout, and turned to meet her eyes across the room, she found herself waiting for his next words with a combination of excitement and trepidation.

"Did you mean what you said this morning?"

Those hadn't been quite the words she'd been expecting. "Mean what?" Kelly asked blankly.

"About getting married the first of next week."

"Oh, that." She bit her lip and then said honestly, "I was feeling provoked at the time." She wasn't at all certain now that she wanted to push the issue. It had been a way of going on the offensive and forcing him to retreat.

"I know you were," he said impatiently. "My question is, if I take you up on it, will you try to run out on me at the last minute? I had more or less told myself after I took you home last night that I needed to give you a little time to get used to the idea of marriage."

"Generous of you," she mocked sarcastically. "Are you sure it isn't yourself who needs the time? Would you run out on me if I agreed to a quick marriage?"

A slow grin crossed his rugged face. "When you look at me like that, how can I do anything but accept the challenge? Come on, honey. Let's go home, have a glass of wine, a good meal, and see which of us backs down first!"

For the life of her, Kelly couldn't explain her own lightheartedness or the accompanying light-headedness. Desperately she made herself say very firmly, "I'm not going to spend the night with you, Locke!"

"Backing down already?"

"Goading me isn't going to work," she drawled tauntingly.

His grin twisted slightly. "What if I promised not to lay a hand on you?"

She blinked warily. "Are you promising that?"

"I got most of what I wanted last night," he told her softly, eyes gleaming. "I can afford to relax some of the pressure."

"Your ego defies description," she said admiringly, knowing the excitement was building between them even as he agreed not to push her back into bed.

"Somehow you never seem short of words when it comes to illustrating it, however," he sighed ruefully. He stood up and picked up the corduroy jacket. "Let's go. You have my word as a fencer and a gentleman that I'll play by your rules tonight."

Much later that evening Kelly, who had been harboring some thrilling inner doubts, was forced to admit that Locke appeared to have every intention of sticking by his word.

She helped him stack the last of the dishes in the dishwasher and wondered despairingly exactly what sort of game he was playing. The evening, she thought in some confusion, had been downright pleasant. They had puttered around the kitchen together, discussing the details of the inventory problem while preparing cracked crab and artichokes.

It was difficult not to get caught up in the intricacies of the programming mystery Locke had uncovered. Even if she'd had no personal interest in the matter, Kelly knew she would have found the conversation irresistible. There was something very beguiling about Locke's enthusiasm for his work. Neither of them mentioned her own tiptoeing through the computer. A truce was in effect.

Now, as they cleared away the remains of the crab and wandered back out into the living room, Kelly felt her pulse stir in spite of her firm determination not to lose control over the evening. She sank into the couch, her jeaned legs stretched out in front of her, and watched as Locke expertly built a fire in the massive stone fireplace.

"Did you build this place yourself?" she asked, glancing up at the heavy beamed ceilings. How much had he told Helen? *How much?*

"I had it built a couple of years ago." He shot a glance up at her from his position on one knee in front of the incipient blaze. "No, I didn't have a wife in mind when I did it."

"You know very well I'd never lower myself to ask that sort of question."

"I know. Thought I'd make it easy for you." He got to his feet and joined her on the couch, sliding down beside her with a relaxed-sounding sigh. "I'm willing to make it all very easy for you, Kelly," he added gently.

"Are you?" She turned her head, which was resting on the back of the couch, to meet the jade gaze.

"Yes."

The sensual tension that had been flowing between them flickered a little brighter as Kelly watched the play of shadows on his face. He'd turned off most of the lights before starting the fire and now its glow was the chief source of illumination.

"No pressure tonight?" she whispered huskily, aware of the tingling in her lower abdomen. Why was this the man who could cause that sensation with only a glance? And last night . . . last night had been unlike anything she had ever known. It made the breath catch in her throat just to think about it.

"The evening is yours." He smiled with perfectly leashed sexual menace. "But I can ask for a kiss, can't I?" The long dark lashes hooded the heated green coals of his eyes. He didn't move, simply sat there with his hands shoved into the front pockets of his jeans and waited with a lazy threat that was not a threat.

"Are you asking?"

"I'm begging," he rasped gently, not bothering to hide the yearning in his words.

Kelly moistened her lips. She didn't know what game he was playing tonight, didn't want to try and decipher it. Whatever it was, it seemed in that moment that two could play.

Without a word she leaned forward and brushed his waiting mouth with her own, her fingertip lightly touching his cheek.

The response was warm and electric without being startling. His lips moved softly, coaxingly, pleadingly, beneath hers, and without being entirely aware of what she was doing, Kelly deepened the kiss.

He was two men, she thought dizzily, the passionate, aggressive lover of last night and the equally sensuous, persuasive lover of tonight. Which was the real Locke? Or were his actions two ends of a spectrum?

Unable to resist the one who sat beside her this evening, Kelly wound her arms around his neck and barely noticed when he scooped her close and settled her softly down on the thick rug in front of the flames.

CHAPTER SEVEN

It was as she felt the softness of the rug beneath her back and opened sensuously heavy eyelids to meet the descending jade-green gaze that Kelly dimly caught sight of the crossed foils hanging on the wall. They stirred her memory. There was a reason she was doing this. A reason she was encouraging Locke's lovemaking.

They were dueling, she reminded herself, feeling the beginnings of helplessness. He wanted something from her, and she wanted something from him. She had to know how much he had told Helen.

But it was difficult to think with the warmth of the flames and the heat of Locke's body crowding in on her.

"Kelly, my sweet little adversary, tell me the truth. You know you became mine last night, don't you?"

Kelly heard the gentle command in the thick silk of his words and could only stare, wide-eyed, up at him as he lowered himself alongside her on the rug.

"Locke, oh, Locke. I think you are a sorcerer at times," she breathed, her fingers finding the heavy darkness of his hair and sliding to his nape.

"I'll become anything it takes to hold you," he vowed huskily.

His hands began to move exploringly, tantalizingly, on her body. It was different tonight, Kelly thought vaguely as her skin responded at all the points of contact. Last night had been wild, the lovemaking fraught with Locke's masculine aggression and his desire to confirm his victory on the most fundamental of levels. She had responded to it with the unexpected wildness she had discovered in herself.

But tonight he was all seduction. Passion and gentleness. Desire and pleading. It was very male, but the emotions and need in him were new to Kelly. She knew instinctively that Locke made love with a passion that probably didn't exist in men like Brett Forrester. Her black-haired, green-eyed lover involved himself totally in the moment, giving all of himself even as he demanded everything in return.

Giving all of himself . . . The words ran through her mind even as his hands and lips moved over her, searching out the sensitive places, claiming them once again. *All of himself.*

Could a man who gave all of himself, even for this short span of time, deliberately hurt the woman he held in his arms? How much had he told Helen? Dear God! How much had he told Helen?

She tried to keep that thought in her mind, determined now to ask it when he was at his weakest. But it was she who was weakening. . . .

"Tonight I shall have the one pleasure I didn't have last night," Locke murmured, his hand stroking down her jeaned leg to encircle her ankle.

"What pleasure?" she asked, aware of the erotic sensation of being lightly bound as he tugged her foot closer.

"Undressing you," he chuckled softly, throatily. Deliberately he slipped off her shoe. "The anticipation makes me ache, but I can't bear to hurry it!"

He unwrapped her as if she were a precious package, and almost unconsciously Kelly did the same to him.

"Locke," she gasped huskily as he slowly unbuttoned her long-sleeved plaid shirt and lightly teased the skin

113

between her unconfined breasts. "I won't stay the night. I only want . . ."

"Yes, sweetheart," he murmured, trailing his fingertips down to her stomach but not yet pushing aside the shirt. "What is it you want? The same thing I want?"

"I want to know—I mean, I want you to tell me about —" She couldn't get the question out!

"Tell you how much I love you? Gladly!" He bent his dark head to nuzzle aside the plaid fabric and let his lips encounter the tips of her breasts in a seemingly random fashion that made her twist beneath him.

"I love you," he went on, groaning his delight in her reaction. "You belong to me now and I'm going to go on loving you until you're dizzy with it!" He slid the jeans down over her hips, eyes heating at the sight of her.

That wouldn't take much, she thought dazedly, her fingers clawing softly at his shirt as she sought the buttons there. Last night his sexual fencing had been relentless. Tonight it was a teasing, provoking thing that was going to drive her insane.

"I don't understand it," she confessed on the sheerest of whispers. "But you make me—" She swallowed, seeking the right word to explain the sensation. "You make me *burn*!"

"Does that frighten you?" he grated, his lips gentle and delicate on first her waist and then her thigh.

"It's—it's different. . . ."

"Because you and I are different. Together we're something unique. Don't you understand that yet?"

"Oh!" The cry came softly as he interrupted the exquisitely sensitive pattern of his lovemaking to close his teeth on the skin of her thigh in a surprisingly sharp bite. The small pain, surrounded as it had been by the soft silk of his mouth, nearly drove her wild.

She must remember her plan, Kelly told herself in a relentless, repetitive way that was rapidly losing all coher-

114

ent meaning. She must ask her question when he would be too weak to do anything else but answer it.

"Look at you," he growled with warm, pleased laughter as she arched against his hand. "You were made for me to love! Your body knows my touch. I want to make it so, that you couldn't bear to have it touched by any other man."

"What about you, Locke?" she demanded thickly as her fingertips found the entrancing hair of his chest. "Do you respond to my touch?"

"Good Lord! Do you need to ask?" he groaned, pressing himself against her hip and leaving her in little doubt about his arousal.

The blatant maleness seemed to impact her senses in a new way, calling to her femininity with the desperate, driving demand of a man who is sure of what he wants and has it within his grasp.

"Finish undressing me, sweetheart," he begged. "I need the feel of your hands on me." Impatiently he unzipped his jeans.

She responded to the sensuous plea, slipping her fingers inside the denim and pushing it downward. In another moment they both lay naked, except for the unbuttoned shirts they were still wearing.

Locke slid his hands inside the opening of Kelly's remaining garment, his fingers working their way up and down her spine in a motion that made her writhe like a cat.

Lying on her side, curled into him, she stroked the line of his ribs down to the male hips and beyond. Her fingers found the base of his spine and probed.

"You have the power to drive me absolutely wild with only a touch," he rasped heavily, his lower body inclining toward her, seeking even greater intimacy. "Tell me I can do the same to you, Kelly, my love. Please tell me!"

She couldn't deny him the admission. It was nothing less than the truth.

"Do you need the words? Can't you feel what's happening to me?" she begged, heedless of the sultry provoking quality of her voice. Her body used it the way it used every other part of itself tonight: as just another lure.

"I can feel your warmth and the softness of your thighs," he admitted, his lips moving on the small rounded breasts. "Your legs wrap around mine as if you won't let me escape. Is that the way you feel?"

"Yes!" It was true, she realized, her head moving restlessly on the rug as he strung deepening kisses up from her nipples to the base of her throat. She couldn't let him go. Not tonight, not ever! What had happened to her?

"Good," he breathed, the single word heavy with masculine possession and satisfaction. "Because that's the way it has to be between us. I can't ever let you go, and this kind of bondage has to be mutual."

"Bondage?" she teased in that new, deeply sexy voice that came with unexpected naturalness tonight. "Are you going to tie me down, dear Locke?"

He raised his head to smile a little savagely down into her glittering silver-blue eyes. The green gems of his own gaze flamed. "Shall I show you how?" he invited.

"Yes, please," she murmured recklessly, her fingers kneading the sleek muscles of his shoulders.

"I always fence to win," he reminded her carefully.

"Losing your nerve?" she taunted, letting the tip of her tongue touch her upper lip in a small exceedingly provocative fashion.

"What do you think?"

"I think you're waiting to see how far I'll goad you." She smiled languidly.

"I don't need any pushing in that direction," he vowed. He bent his head to kiss the base of her ear and then delicately bit the lobe.

116

Kelly moaned softly, her legs twisting as the sensual throbbing shot through her.

"Watch this," he instructed in a sexy growl.

"Huh? Oh!"

He threw a rough male thigh across her legs, stilling the restlessness of her limbs, while his lips took their fill of her breasts again. Her hands were carefully caught and held at her sides.

Then he shifted, poising himself above her, letting her become aware of his strength and power in the farthest recesses of her mind and body. Slowly he lowered himself until he lay along the whole length of her, not yet completing the union but filling her with the inevitability of that completion.

"I can't move," she half laughed, half protested. He was using his weight and his legs and his hands to chain her completely on the rug beneath him.

"I like to see you a little helpless now and then," he murmured outrageously, kissing her throat and eyelids and cheeks in deliberate, heated caresses.

"Does that please your male ego?" she charged, enormously aware of the scorching intimacy of his hips as they ground hers into the rug. For all its plushness, the rug wasn't providing much cushioning under their combined weights. She was breathing quickly now, waiting for the moment when he completely mastered her body with his own.

"Knowing you're mine pleases my male ego enormously," he confirmed with passionate mockery.

"But you can't move either," she pointed out huskily. "To hold me helpless means to hold me completely."

"Now do you understand?" he whispered. "You can't have a fencing match without two opponents. You can't have a love affair without two lovers. . . ."

"But a love affair doesn't always require love," she said

breathlessly, eyes searching his face. "Other emotions can bring two people together like this."

"Don't you think I know that? Other emotions like desire and need can draw them together but can't hold them together. I love you, Kelly. I've put my bonds on you. Those bonds are strong. They'll have to be strong enough to hold us like this until you realize you're in love with me."

She heard the utter determination in his voice and felt the shock of it throughout her whole system. Was it possible? Did her green-eyed warlock really love her? She knew as they lay there in incredible intimacy that she had succumbed to his power last night. There could be no doubt. She had fallen in love with the man who could destroy her.

"You look shaken, sweetheart," he muttered, sounding pleased. He nibbled on her shoulder almost playfully. "You're having a hard time comprehending the fact that a man who wants only you has fallen in love with you."

"Is that all you want?" She waited tensely for his answer, every nerve and fiber taut. "Is that really all you want?"

"You wouldn't ask that if you knew how completely I wanted you," he told her fervently. "Has anyone ever wanted you, body and soul? Has any man known what it means to tear down every one of your brilliant defenses and take the real you behind them?"

"You're asking if I've ever been totally and completely in love, aren't you?"

"I think I know the answer already," he said whimsically, green eyes flaring. "It's no. If you had been, you would have recognized what was happening to you this time around. You wouldn't be fighting it so hard."

"Does that mean you have known what it feels like?" Kelly couldn't deny the pain of that thought. She didn't want there to have ever been a passionate, head-over-heels sort of love in his life. A strange, irrational jealousy swamped her at the thought.

"No," he said at once, sounding quite firm and enormously reassuring. "There's never been anything else like this for me. Why do you think I leaped to grab it with both hands? I recognized it because I'm the logical thinker you've accused me of being," he added with a rich chuckle.

"You're so very sure of yourself. . . ."

"If you mean I'm very sure of wanting you, then, yes, I'm certain of myself!"

"Will you give as much in return?" she asked painfully.

"I'm a man, sweetheart," he grated against her mouth. "I only know one way to show you how much of me I'm willing to give!"

She gasped as he found the warmth between her legs, taking her with the sweet, driving aggression she had first learned last night, but not rushing the rhythm of this match.

This time the fencing of their bodies and minds was a slow, rippling, astoundingly sensual thing. It was as if they made love in another medium or on another plane. It was delicious, tantalizing, overpoweringly controlled.

Too controlled, Kelly thought as her body began to attempt a shift in the thrust and parry of their sexual swordplay. She felt her feverish reactions begin to go beyond what Locke was permitting.

"Locke," she panted as he forced her to follow his lead. "Locke, please!"

"Fight back, little one," he breathed heavily in her ear. "Let me see how strong you really are!"

She answered the challenge with a small cry of feminine aggression—an aggression she was only beginning to comprehend. It was the sensual equivalent of the power and need to win she felt when she held a foil in her gloved hand.

Far back in the most primitive, female core of her, she must have known about this other kind of power. It must have always been there, lying dormant within, waiting for the male counterpart to draw it forth.

She fought the man who had stirred it alive, fought him for the embrace and for control of the passion. But he wouldn't relinquish it easily. He made that clear with his exciting strength and mastery. Deliberately he dared her to assume control.

With the wild abandon sweeping over her once again, Kelly came fully alive in Locke's arms. She gave herself up to the raging need inside, and the more she surrendered to it, the more power seemed to flow from it.

"Kelly! My God, woman!"

"Love me! Please, love me!" she cried, unaware of the way her nails were scoring his back.

And he did. Together they fought the primitive love battle to its inevitable conclusion, a conclusion that left them soaring one moment on the wave of victory and then hurled them to the mat in a damp, tangled heap.

For a long time Kelly lay in the quiet aftermath with Locke sprawled half across her replete body. His dark head was lying alongside her own, his breathing hoarse and reviving.

She stared at the crossed foils on the wall behind the couch and tried to remember why she had allowed the lovemaking to begin earlier. There had been a point to it, she knew. A question waited that must be asked.

"What are you thinking, sweetheart?" Locke asked quietly, his lips brushing her shoulder lazily.

"I was waiting for you to tell me you're hungry," she teased, mentally shying away from asking the crucial question. She had wanted to put it to him when he was at his weakest. She had meant to do it before things had gone this far. Now it was too late. Things *had* gone too far and she couldn't formulate the words.

120

"I will be in a few minutes," he smiled imperturbably.

"You know yourself very well, don't you?"

"It's the way I think, I suppose," he admitted with a long sleepy sigh.

"Logically?"

"Ummm."

"Have you ever done anything that was illogical?"

"Sure. Everyone does. But I always know when I'm doing it. I sort of stand back and watch myself indulgently."

"Illogic is an indulgence?"

"Are we playing psychologist tonight?" He grinned, green eyes lighting with humor.

"Aren't you pleased that I find your conversation interesting?" she taunted.

He laughed outright at that. "Every man wants to be loved for his mind as well as his sex appeal."

"Your modesty overwhelms me."

"Don't worry. The admiration is mutual. I thoroughly delight in your conversation too!"

"I suppose that's reassuring. I wouldn't like to think you were only interested in me as a built-in fencing partner."

Kelly turned lovingly in his arms and gasped in unexpected discomfort.

"Ouch!"

"What's wrong, sweetheart?" Locke levered himself up on an elbow to examine her worriedly.

"I must make sure you get in the habit of using beds for this sort of thing," she muttered, putting a hand to the rounded portion of her anatomy, which had taken the brunt of their combined weight against the rug.

"Oh, I see." He smiled wickedly, his eyes following her movement. "If it makes you feel any better, I'm going to be carrying a few scars too!"

"What scars? I was the one providing the cushioning effect!" she complained, sitting up very carefully.

"But you weren't wearing gloves," he pointed out, lifting probing fingers to his shoulders.

Kelly bit her lip and dissolved into unrepentant giggles. "Consider yourself branded."

"I will," he said instantly, lowering his hand to snag her around the waist and tug her close. "We've both put our marks on each other tonight," he added on a whisper as he cradled her against his chest. "I've no complaints."

"Masochist!"

"Probably." There was a small pause and she felt him take a deep breath before going on. "Kelly?"

"What is it, Locke?"

"I have to know. . . ."

"Know what?" She wasn't thinking about anything except the warm, loving feel of him, and it was difficult to concentrate.

"I have to know why you did what you did."

"Just now? I'm not sure I can put it into words. . . ."

"No, sweetheart." His voice lowered and she knew his lips were in the braided coil of her hair, which had come undone. "I want you to tell me why you went into the computer and did what you did."

Kelly dragged her languid senses back into startled awareness of what was happening. It wasn't fair! she thought, appalled. She hadn't had the ability to go after her own answers tonight, but he quite calmly was pursuing his investigation as if nothing had happened between them. Anger poured through her veins—a hot, irrational anger that made her first freeze and then burn.

"How could you!" she ripped out, yanking herself away from him. His hands fell aside in response to her abrupt action. "How dare you do this to me!"

"Kelly, calm down! Wait a minute! Let me explain!"

But she was already on her feet, clutching the plaid shirt closed and reaching for the pile of jeans and underwear. Holding them in front of her, she glared at him, her eyes chips of flaming ice as the braid fell forward across her shoulder. She felt so horribly vulnerable!

"All that talk of love and—and making me yours! It was so much garbage, wasn't it? And I almost fell for it. I almost believed you this time, Locke Channing! Do you realize that? How close I came to trusting you? I'll never forgive you for doing this to me."

"Will you quiet down and listen to me, you little fool?" he snapped, heaving himself to his feet in a single coordinated bound. He faced her, hands on hips, making no effort to cover his own nakedness.

"That's exactly what I've been the past couple of days. A fool. But there's a cure for that degree of stupidity and you just administered it yourself."

Fumbling, she stooped to pull on her jeans, feeling the need to have the protection of her clothes.

"Kelly, I need the answer to that question. Don't you understand, sweetheart?" Locke stepped forward, yanking her erect before she could fasten the snap of her jeans. Fingers digging into her shoulders, he forced her to meet his determined eyes.

"I had a question of my own tonight, Locke. Did you realize that?" she gritted in self-mockery. "I kissed you tonight because I had some crazy idea I could persuade you to give me my answer."

"Ask it, honey. Just ask it."

"I can't! Not now! Now I wouldn't know whether or not you were lying to me, would I? I really became your defeated victim tonight, didn't I? I let go by the chance I might have had to get a truthful answer from you because I let myself get seduced again. What's the matter with me? What in the name of heaven makes a woman fall for a man who's out to destroy her?" The last words were almost a wail of fury and regret and self-disgust.

"Destroy you? Kelly, what are you talking about, you demented female? I'm not out to destroy you. That's the last thing on earth I would want to do. I want to protect you."

"A fine protection!" she hissed, eyes slitting with anger and hurt. "You seduced me so that you can persuade me to give you the answer to your precious investigation. Well, you can damn well keep investigating, Locke, because I'm not going to risk becoming this weakened again. You had your chance and you blew it. You probably should have asked me a little earlier, before I'd had a chance to recover. That's what I was going to do with you. Ask my question while you were in the throes of passion. What a laugh! I couldn't even think straight enough to get the words out."

"Do you imagine I was in any shape to get my question out while holding you? All I could think about was wanting you, needing you!"

"Then it's a standoff, isn't it? We've fought each other to a standstill tonight. Thank you for telling me that much at least. I'll have the satisfaction of knowing your plans didn't come off any better than mine did."

She whirled, intent only on making for the door.

"Where do you think you're going?" he barked, reaching out to snag a wrist and halt her progress.

"Home."

"How?"

"I'll drive myself if you won't do it."

"I'm not driving you anywhere. We're going to have this out."

"The hell we are," she stated with frightening sweetness, holding out her palm. "Give me the keys."

He reached down to grab his jeans, pulling the keys out

of the back pocket and clasping them firmly in his free hand. "Not a chance!"

"Why you . . . !"

"Say it and I'll probably wind up beating you tonight! You're having a disastrous effect on my temper!"

Stormy silver-blue eyes clashed for a silent tense moment with warlock green, and Kelly knew beyond a shadow of a doubt he meant what he said. She had about as much chance of getting her hands on those keys as she had of reprogramming the Forrester computer!

"Where's all that fine love and romance you were vowing a little while ago?" she taunted recklessly. "What's the matter? Are you finding that your feelings weren't quite as strong as you thought?"

"Loving you won't prevent me from giving you what you're asking for this evening," he swore, his fingers tightening on her wrist. "You're going to spend the night here, Kelly Winfield. Resign yourself to it!"

She considered that, her head high, chin tilted defiantly. "Very well," she declared aloofly. "Since you're going back on your word, I don't seem to have much choice."

"What word?" he grated angrily.

"You said you would play by my rules tonight. Forgotten already? Typical!"

"You can't blame a man for failing to act the gentleman when you push him as far as you've pushed me!"

"Could we skip the excuses?"

"We can skip the excuses, but not the questions! What was it you were going to seduce me into telling you, Kelly?"

The deep metal and silk voice was entirely metallic-sounding. He meant to have an answer.

"If I ask my question, will you let me go?" she snapped, a vague sort of plan forming in the back of her mind.

"I won't let you go home, but I'll let go of your wrist, yes."

"Damned decent of you!"

"Isn't it, though?" he said between clenched teeth. "Ask your question!"

"Okay," she muttered, attempting an uncaring lift of her shoulders. "If that's what you want."

"It is."

"I was going to ask you how much you told Helen." There. It was out. He would probably lie to her, naturally, but at least the burning question had been asked. If only she would know how to interpret his answer. So much depended on it. . . .

He looked a little blank. It disconcerted her. "How much have I told Helen about what? About us?"

"No, about what I did to the computer," she blazed, infuriated.

"Oh, that."

"Don't you dare laugh at me!"

"I can't help it," he admitted on a groan of poorly suppressed humor. "Of all the stupid—"

"Just answer the question!" she raged.

"I haven't told her a damn thing! Why should I?" he shot back, shaking his head reprovingly.

"You didn't go to her when you found out what I'd done? She didn't ask you to determine why I'd messed about with the data?" She mustn't believe him. He was lying!

"My God, you're becoming a thoroughgoing paranoid, aren't you? Is this why you've been so edgy all day? You thought I was laying a trap for you?"

"Aren't you?" It was almost a squeak. In spite of herself Kelly was staring at him with hope in her eyes.

"The only trap I've set for you you've already fallen into. I just haven't shut the door completely behind you yet."

"You would be an easy man to strangle!"

"You have to catch me first." He grinned, tugging her

closer. The irritation was fading from the jade eyes to be replaced with male laughter. "But I'll make that easy for you too. I've told you I'm not out to complicate things, sweetheart. Simple is logical."

Fiercely aware of his continuing nakedness in the face of her now-dressed condition, Kelly struggled in annoyance.

"Locke . . ."

"It's time for my question, honey," he reminded her gently, wrapping his arms around her waist and pressing her unself-consciously to his warm nudity. "Why? Tell me why and we can have done with this crazy argument."

She stiffened, her hands pushing unsuccessfully against his shoulders. "Is the answer so important to you?" she heard herself ask bemusedly.

"Yes."

"Why?"

"Because if you answer it, I'll know you trust me, won't I?"

"And if you know that?" she prodded uncertainly.

"I'll know you love me."

Jolted, she froze for an instant. If only she could think properly. But her head seemed to be spinning. She needed time. Time to consider the truth and sort out the lies. Life was becoming a morass of wheels within wheels and it was all because of this man. Could she believe him?"

"Knowing I love you would give you the final victory, wouldn't it?" she whispered meditatively, unable to look away from the intense green gems of his eyes. The firm mouth hardened as he studied her.

"It would." He made no attempt to deny it.

"And if I made an error in judgment, trusted you when I shouldn't, I would be giving you a weapon."

"Yes." She sensed the leashed tension in him and marveled at it. Instinct told her he wanted to pounce, tear aside her qualms, and demand his answer.

"That doesn't sound very bright on my part," she made herself retort sarcastically.

"It sounds very *trusting*. . . ."

"I have to decide whether you want the answer in order to solve your problem with the computer investigation or because you really want my love and nothing else."

He sighed. "You've surely been burned in the past, haven't you?"

"I've survived," she managed flippantly.

"The only thing I want is you, sweetheart. Take a chance. Trust me and find out. . . ."

She wrenched herself free of the persuasive feel of his arms, away from the coaxing, cajoling gleam in his eyes. Without giving it a thought, she ran lightly to the stairs and up to the landing. At the top she paused for an instant to look down at him. He seemed quite pagan standing naked in front of the fire. He was watching her intently.

"You still won't agree to drive me home tonight?" she demanded loftily.

"No."

"Then I'll see you in the morning!" She stepped inside his bedroom, then slammed and locked the door.

CHAPTER EIGHT

It was the precarious sound of a rattling teacup that woke Kelly early the next morning. For a painful moment after opening her bleary eyes she lay where she was, an unmoving sprawl across Locke's bed.

With unpleasant suddenness the events of the previous evening returned and the whirling thoughts and arguments that had kept her awake half the night were lying in wait, prepared to renew the fray. She eyed the expanse of white sheet in dismay. Locke Channing's bed.

"Never let it be said I don't know how to treat a guest. Breakfast in bed, no less!" Locke's voice came, unbelievably cheery, and when Kelly shifted her gaze a matter of inches, she caught sight of a pair of dark slacks standing beside the bed.

"I locked that door. I distinctly remember doing it," she muttered forcefully, saying the first words that came into her head.

"This is my house, remember?" he retorted gently. "I've got keys to all the doors."

She thought about that, still gazing across the sheet at the dark slacks. "You didn't use the key to get in last night," she finally observed with a curious sense of detachment.

"Something told me you wouldn't be exactly welcoming. Besides, I had a couple of things to do."

"I heard you getting into the refrigerator," she accused.

"I've told you I get hungry after—"

"Have you really got some tea on that tray?" she interrupted feelingly, turning onto her side to view him from behind a mild glare.

"Tea and English muffins and an egg. What more could a woman ask?"

"You may be right."

Kelly began to struggle into a sitting position against the pillows, realized belatedly she had nothing on, and promptly slumped back.

"Would you mind handing me my shirt?" she asked with gritty politeness.

"Whatever my lady wishes." He set down the tray on the bedside table and scooped up the shirt she had tossed onto a nearby chair. He threw it toward her with a grin.

"Please turn around," she ordered haughtily, not appreciating the humor in his eyes. How could he look so pleased with himself after last night? Then again, why shouldn't he? She'd made a fool out of herself, hadn't she?

He obediently turned his back to her, not coming around until he heard her pick up the tray. Then he stood there, black hair still damp from the shower, shirt unbuttoned at the collar, and smiled affectionately as she wolfed down the meal.

"Hungry, huh? You should have come back downstairs when you heard me in the refrigerator last night."

"I had some thinking to do," she announced coolly around a bite of English muffin.

He walked forward and flung himself down onto the foot of the bed, facing her with an expression of great interest, his hands folded across his chest. "Come to any conclusions?"

"If you haven't told Helen about what you found . . ." she began determinedly.

"I haven't."

"And I can safely assume you're not planning to trap

130

me into telling you why I did it just so you'll have the satisfaction of finding the motive . . ."

"You trust me that far at least?" One dark brow lifted interrogatively.

"I'm outlining possibilities," she told him evenly, shooting him a narrow glance.

"Okay. If I haven't told Helen . . . ?"

"Then are you still going to use the threat of telling her to get me to marry you?" She made the question sound very casual. It took an effort.

"Will I need to?" he countered, equally blandly.

Kelly made herself take a deep, steadying breath before answering.

"If you're serious about marrying me . . ."

"I am."

"I'll agree to it on two conditions. The first is that you keep your word and don't tell Helen about what you found in the computer."

"And the second?" he encouraged with a hint of wariness.

"And the second is that you don't demand any more answers from me before the wedding."

She stopped chewing, waiting in an agony of suspense for his reaction. She was unaware of the anxiety in the silvery blue eyes that watched him with such tense anticipation.

He took a long time answering. Kelly thought she would go crazy waiting for his response. It had taken all night to formulate her simple plan. And all he had to do to defeat it was refuse to accept the conditions she had placed on the marriage.

"I have no intention of telling Helen," he stated slowly, as if choosing his words. There was a distinct tension at the corners of his mouth, Kelly saw, wondering what he was thinking. "But do you realize just what you're asking with that second condition?"

131

"I'm asking you to prove you mean what you say. That you do want to marry me and that you're not pretending to love me in order to seduce me into giving you the solution to your stupid little mystery."

"That's looking at it from your point of view," he noted calmly. "I see it slightly differently. What you're really asking me to do is marry you with no guarantees that the reason you're going through with the marriage is because you care for me, perhaps even love me. You might very well be trying to buy my silence because you're so afraid of having the truth about those computer transactions come out."

Kelly lifted her head proudly, her soft brown hair streaming down her back and shoulders. The silver-blue eyes flashed angrily as she faced him. "I'm not *afraid* of anything! But it would be vastly more convenient for all concerned if you didn't go to Helen with your tale. And I have no wish to take the risk of telling you the whole story and finding out too late you were only trying to trick me, after all! If you marry me, I'll tell you what you want to know after the wedding."

"You mean after I've proved I was sincere."

"Yes."

"When do I get my proof?" he asked softly.

She bit her lip. "I've told you. I'll tell you the full story after the wedding."

"Maybe you will and maybe you won't. Either way it won't prove much, will it? If you tell me the truth after the wedding, it will only prove you're willing to carry out your end of the conditions you set on the marriage. It won't prove that you trust me or love me."

"Somehow this is getting very complicated," she protested in growing frustration.

"Only because you're not looking at the whole thing logically," he assured her gently. "I asked you to marry me—"

"Tried to coerce me into marriage, you mean!"

"Whatever you say," he admitted agreeably. "At any rate I confess that, although I intended to marry you, I also intended to get the story surrounding that computer caper first. I'm not a complete masochist, Kelly. I want to go into my marriage with some assurance that my bride is as in love with me as I am with her."

"It must have come as a shock when I started talking about setting the wedding date for early next week," she muttered a little nastily.

"It did. But I figured that might be a positive sign. It does mean I have to get my answer fairly quickly, though, doesn't it?" He smiled wryly.

She sighed dejectedly, staring down at her half-eaten egg. "You won't marry me if I don't prove I trust you, is that it?"

There was a lengthy pause from the foot of the bed. "Don't pin me down," Locke finally said ruefully, a statement that brought Kelly's head up with a snap. "I may get desperate enough to take the risk. I'm hoping it won't come to that. I'd like very much to marry a woman who could look me in the eye and say she trusted me and loved me."

Kelly couldn't find any words to answer that. Put that way, it sounded so reasonable . . . so *logical!*

Locke's mouth quirked upward as he saw her expression. "You were wrong a few minutes ago, honey. You *are* afraid of something, aren't you? Why don't you admit it? You're afraid of asking a man to share your problems. You're so used to shouldering the entire responsibility, so used to being the strong one, that you've become frightened of sharing. No one can be strong all the time, sweetheart. The trick is to mesh your strength with someone who is every bit as strong as you are."

"You?" she suggested bleakly, alarmed at the way his logic was beginning to make sense to her.

"Me. Now eat your breakfast and stop worrying about things for a while. I understand we have a party to attend this evening."

Kelly looked up again, startled. "I forgot to mention it. . . ."

"Lucky for me I saw Helen in the hall yesterday, huh? I might not have had time to get my tux pressed."

Kelly couldn't fight back her slow grin. "Corduroy jackets being the latest thing in evening wear?"

"I knew my fashion consciousness would attract you sooner or later." He got to his feet in a lithe movement.

"Locke?" Her voice halted him at the door and she waited as he turned to glance back at her over his shoulder. "What makes you such an authority on my—er—problem?"

His face softened. "Haven't you guessed that much yet? I've suffered from the same difficulty for thirty-five years. The only difference between us is that I've managed to look at it objectively."

"Reasoned out the problem in a logical manner?" she couldn't resist saying goadingly.

"Don't feel bad. Given another four or five years, you probably would have come to similar conclusions about yourself. As it happens, I don't care to wait that long!"

"What did you decide to do after you realized your—uh—situation?" Kelly demanded coolly.

"Oh, that was simple enough. I started looking around for someone who could understand me." He shut the door behind him, the essence of his grin staying behind to warm the room.

Kelly dressed with care for Helen's cocktail party that evening. She went through the female rituals with an abstracted air of decision, taking some comfort in the process. Her brown hair, brushed until the red and gold in it shone, was parted in the middle again and bound into a smooth coil at the nape.

After much perusal of the contents of her closet, she selected a clinging sapphire-blue dress styled with long tight-fitting sleeves and a high neck that opened to a daring point just above her breasts. The blue material had a deepening effect on the color of her eyes, and the slender, elegant lines seemed to highlight her supple fencer's body.

She studied herself rigorously in the brass-trimmed mirror, satisfied with the overall effect. She looked aloof, icy, and in complete control of her own destiny. Only her escort would know otherwise, she thought grimly.

Locke had taken her home after feeding her breakfast that morning, leaving her alone with instructions not to drive herself crazy trying to think about the situation in which she found herself. Easy for him to say! It nettled her that he seemed so unconcerned about her dilemma. But then he probably didn't have that same sense of time running out as she did. After all, he hadn't committed himself to the marriage quite the way she had. . . .

She shied away from that thought in relief as the doorbell sounded, aware of a certain dampening of her palms as she went forward to answer it.

"Good heavens! I almost didn't recognize you," she forced herself to say very brightly as she viewed the unexpected apparition on her doorstep. "Did someone steal your jacket?"

Locke contrived to look reproachful, glancing self-consciously down his own length. "Unkind. I spent an hour searching for this today. I'd forgotten which closet I'd hung it in."

"Well, if it makes you feel any better, it was worth the hunt. You look—" Kelly broke off, feeling like an idiot. But he did look almost terrifyingly attractive to her tonight. The dark well-cut jacket and trousers were accented by a brilliantly white silk shirt and richly hued tie. The gun-metal black of his hair lay in a thick tidy pelt, contributing to the overall effect of dangerous darkness. The

135

jade-green eyes were fierce lures in his tanned face. He looked more like a warlock than ever.

"Yes?" he encouraged helpfully, flashing a slightly menacing grin. "How do I look?"

"I have a feeling you already know the answer to that," she shot back dryly.

"Like your nemesis, hmmm?"

"Is that how you see yourself?" she retorted, turning away to pick up her small silver evening bag.

"Lately I've tended to view myself as you view me." He chuckled, coming forward to help her slip the warm white wool shawl over her shoulders. "It's useful for strategy purposes."

Kelly parted her lips to parry with a sharp retort, but he silenced her words with a finger on her mouth.

"You, on the other hand, look very lovely tonight, my sweet little opponent," he went on in a dark nerve-riflingly sexy voice. The green eyes gleamed with sheer masculine promise and approval. "Cool, a bit haughty, and heavily posted with no-trespassing signs. I like the fact that only I will know the truth."

"What makes you think the no-trespassing signs don't apply to you too?" she inquired silkily, fighting the tremor of remembered passion that had shivered through her at his nearness.

"Last night makes me think they don't. And if that wasn't enough to convince me, I've always got the evidence of the evening before that to go on!"

Kelly winced. "You may be dressed like a gentleman tonight, but you're not behaving like one! Locke, please," she went on with sudden appeal, her eyes glinting a shade lighter with pleading. "No more—"

"No more reminders of the last two nights?"

She shook her head impatiently. "No. What I'm saying is, no more of what *happened* the last two nights!"

136

"Ah." He nodded in a very knowing tone of voice. "Something else you're afraid of?"

She narrowed her eyes at the hint of male satisfaction in him. "It's not a question of being afraid. It's a question of not being able to think properly," she snapped. "I want time to sort this mess out in a—a *logical* fashion. I'm sure you can appreciate that."

"Oh, I can understand, all right. I go a little crazy when I make love to you too, sweetheart," he murmured tenderly. "I suppose I could look on this as another step in the right direction."

"What do you mean by that?" she asked quellingly.

"You've known from the first night I kissed you that you could call a halt to our lovemaking when you wished. I told you then I'd never resort to rape and I think you believe me. I wouldn't, in the final analysis, have forced you last night or the night before. Ergo, we are left with one conclusion!"

"Ergo?"

"You don't trust yourself to be able to call a halt to the seduction process," he explained with bland certainty. "You're asking me to be the watchdog and temper the lovemaking. Which means—"

"I don't think I want to hear this."

"Which means that in this particular matter you trust my strength more than your own," he concluded triumphantly.

"Oh, my God!" she gritted feelingly, whirling on one high-heeled ankle and striding briskly for the door. "Your thought processes have become too convoluted for even a computer to unravel!"

"You're just jealous," he began complacently, following her to the door. "Hey, that's one hell of a stereo system!"

She glanced over her shoulder at the gleaming components stacked in the wooden cabinet. "What do you expect? I work for a firm that sells them." It was her turn to break off her words. She swallowed uncomfortably. Did he think she might have got the expensive equipment through less than legitimate methods?

"Every job has its perks," Locke observed as he slid her neatly into the black Jag.

"What are the perks of being a computer-security consultant?" she asked a little recklessly, anxious to turn the subject around.

"Getting to work on a breed of machines that represent some of the most sophisticated technology in the world and proving their fallibility is one aspect," he grinned, starting the engine and reversing out of the parking lot. "Something of an ego trip, I expect."

"Any others?" she queried, interested in spite of her precarious mood.

"I like the challenge of having to think as logically as the computer and then using another kind of logic altogether to detect the weaknesses of the machine's reasoning," he admitted, flicking her an amused glance. "Once I'd discovered what I liked doing in life, I had two choices."

"You could either get your kicks being a computer crook yourself or have the fun of outwitting them, right?" she hazarded with an involuntary smile.

"You can think pretty logically yourself when you put your mind to it," he said admiringly.

"Do you suppose it's contagious?" she wondered wryly.

Enough heads turned when Helen opened the door to them to make Kelly wonder if everyone in the room was reacting to the envelope of invisible electricity that seemed to surround herself and Locke that evening.

The knowledge that somehow they had managed not merely to arrive but to make an *entrance* was a bit unnerving. But the speculative glances were polite and Helen's warm greeting masked the momentary discomfort.

"If I had any doubts about this marriage," the older

woman said smilingly as she ushered them into the room, "they've been resolved. Any woman who could get Locke into a tie and evening jacket knows how to manage a man!"

"You look fantastic tonight, Helen," Kelly said quickly, far more relaxed in her boss's presence this evening now that she knew Locke hadn't told her everything. Kelly didn't want to think about her trust in him. It had dawned on her inevitably during that long night alone in his bed and she had realized that morning she believed him on that point at least. Perhaps, she told herself unhappily, because she wanted so badly to believe him.

Helen's graying blond hair looked sophisticated and elegant, and her simple black dress was adequately adorned by diamond pendant and earrings. Years of practice at being the company president's wife had given her an adroit ability to organize a party, which she now used for her own benefit instead of her husband's.

"Do come in, both of you." She smiled cheerfully. "Brett's handling the drinks over by the bar, of course. I think you know several people here tonight, Kelly. And, Locke, I think you'll find a few familiar faces in the crowd."

Kelly was aware of Locke's arm sliding possessively around her waist as he led her off toward the bar. They paused at several points in the crossing of Helen's huge richly antiqued living room to greet friends and accept congratulations on their forthcoming marriage. Word, Kelly realized ruefully, had spread quickly.

"Do you really know many people here?" she asked Locke quietly as they advanced determinedly toward the bar.

"No, only a couple. Helen and I don't circulate in the same crowd. Pity. If we did, I might have met you sooner."

139

"Hi, Kelly," Brett said with commendable enthusiasm. "Locke."

Poor Brett, Kelly thought sadly. He must be in agony, wondering what's going on. She would have to reassure him as soon as possible.

"What will you have?" their host went on cheerily, his gray gaze back on Kelly. Only she could see the uncertainty there.

"Some of that jug wine you're passing off as vintage stuff," she teased, automatically trying to ease his qualms.

"Don't let Helen hear you say that," Brett advised, taking his cue. "She paid a fortune for a whole case of it! Locke?"

"Scotch," Locke said succinctly, not making any effort to be friendly.

Kelly felt his hostility toward the younger man and would like very much to have kicked him. Didn't he realize there was no real threat here? But a man's jealousy wasn't always a logical thing, she reminded herself on a wave of thoughtful hope.

"There's no call to be rude," she hissed at her escort as they moved away from the bar, drinks in hand.

"There's no call to be polite either," he pointed out briefly, swishing the Scotch around the ice and taking a lengthy sip.

"Has anyone ever told you that your overly rational approach to life is going to get you into trouble some day?"

"You have. Several times. Come on, honey, let's mingle. I think I see a familiar face over there in the corner." He took her arm very firmly. "A man I did some work for last fall. . . ."

It was quite a while before Kelly found the opportunity to talk privately to Brett. She seized it at once, leaving Locke to talk shop with a local bank executive. Making a minor excuse, she slipped away and found Brett talking to a handsome older couple in the corner near an elegant Victorian sofa.

"Oh, hello, Kelly. Meet Mr. and Mrs. Bailey. Friends of the family," Brett said politely as she moved closer.

Kelly nearly lost her footing for an instant. Bailey? She knew that name. Amanda Bailey's parents presumably. Mother and father of the mysterious ex-fiancée. . . .

"How do you do?" she managed formally, summoning a polite smile. But there was no indication of resentment in the friendly eyes that smiled at her. Graciously, neither Mr. or Mrs. Bailey made reference to Locke.

"Could I talk to you a moment, Brett?" Kelly finally said quietly when the pleasantries had been properly exchanged.

"Of course. Excuse us, please," Brett said easily to the couple. He moved away with Kelly to a quiet area near the French doors, which opened onto a balcony. "What is it, Kelly? Are things getting bad?"

"Things," Kelly said determinedly, "are up in the air at the moment. But I thought you'd like to know Helen hasn't been told anything about what I did to the data base."

"Whew! That's one heck of a relief," he muttered. "I've been on pins and needles all day, trying to figure out how to go to her and explain."

"You were prepared to do that?" Kelly asked in barely concealed surprise.

"What else could I do? I couldn't let you take the blame. I told you that yesterday," he vowed forcefully.

"That's very—very kind of you, Brett," she said, a little bewildered. She hadn't expected him to be so willing to confess to his parent.

He saw her expression and smiled wryly. "I've done some growing up in the past few months, Kelly. It happens, you know."

"Yes, well . . ."

The new voice that cut in on Kelly's faltering response was full of delightful, bright, tinkling female amusement.

"So there you are, Brett! Good! You can introduce me to the victim who took my place. I've been dying to meet the next brave woman who's going to try and wean Locke Channing away from his computers. Tell me the truth now," Amanda Bailey commanded with charming laughter. "Has the incredible boredom begun to set in yet?" She turned her lovely hazel eyes directly on Kelly.

CHAPTER NINE

"Boredom?" Kelly said quite blankly, mentally trying to reconcile that concept with the warlock who had been pursuing her for the past few days.

Damn, but the woman was beautiful, the hazel eyes slightly slanted and sexy, the seemingly casual blond hair, and a voluptuously full figure with narrow waist and shapely hips. It was all on a delightfully petite frame. Amanda Bailey had probably spent the better part of her life looking up at men with an adoring look. She was that sort of female, Kelly decided vengefully. And she was also only about twenty-four years old. Kelly felt her evening going downhill in a hurry.

Somehow Amanda managed to look quite apologetic in the face of Kelly's confusion.

"I shouldn't have said anything," she confided quickly, laughingly, hazel eyes dancing mischievously. "How long have you been engaged to Locke?" Amanda glanced idly down at Kelly's bare hand.

"Only a day," Kelly said coolly, assessing her opponent. She couldn't help it. That was the way she found herself thinking of Amanda Bailey.

"Oh, well, then, there's plenty of time. I lasted nearly two months myself. Take my advice, though. When the first glimmerings of boredom set in, don't waste your time thinking it's temporary. It won't get any better, only worse!"

"If you don't mind," Kelly began more firmly, her polite smile thinning rapidly, "I think I'll go and find Locke."

"I saw him over there, talking to a banker. Locke gets along well with bankers," Amanda chuckled. "Locke and a banker can spend an entire evening talking about nothing but computer applications to banking! Notice how you're standing here talking to Brett? Whenever I went to a party with Locke, I found myself in the same boat, the only difference being that I wasn't always lucky enough to have Brett to amuse me!"

"I see," Kelly said, a little fascinated by Amanda's cheerful warnings.

"Don't you think you ought to give Kelly and Locke a chance, Amanda?" Brett murmured philosophically. "Just because you and he didn't work out doesn't mean their luck won't be better."

"Perhaps," Amanda conceded with obvious doubt. "And I can certainly understand the initial attraction!" She lifted her hazel eyes heavenward with a reminiscent glance. "Those eyes! They have a way of pinning a woman down and holding her there while Locke decides whether he wants the quarry. Unfortunately the eyes are his only saving grace. The minute he opens his mouth, nothing but computers comes out."

"Locke does seem to enjoy his work," Kelly contributed carefully, flicking a sardonic glance up at Brett, who grimaced.

"That's putting it mildly," Amanda groaned good-naturedly. "Still, looking like he does tonight, all dark and attractive, a woman could find a use for him even if he can't carry on a decent conversation. The thing to do with Locke Channing is have an affair but not tie yourself down to marriage. Take my advice, Kelly. I should have listened to myself."

With a charming little gesture and a dazzling smile for

Brett, Amanda Bailey danced away, leaving the other two staring after her.

"Pretty little thing, isn't she?" Brett finally remarked thoughtfully.

"Oh, very," Kelly agreed dryly. "Ever dated her?"

Brett shook his head, still watching the younger woman as she disappeared into the crowd. "We saw a bit too much of each other while growing up, I guess. I never really thought of her as a potential girl friend. . . ."

"Until tonight?" Kelly hazarded, sipping her wine and watching his expression interestedly.

Brett turned back with a laugh. "I haven't seen her for almost a year. Amazing what can happen in a year!"

"She seems quite—er—gregarious," Kelly noted, watching out of the corner of her eye as the blonde paused to chat briefly with several people. There seemed to be a basic direction behind the apparently random moves around the room, however. In another moment Kelly was sure of it. Amanda was working her way toward Locke and his banker.

"She's always a big hit at parties, as I recall," Brett nodded agreeably. "Everybody loves her." He smiled at Kelly. "Can I get you some more wine?"

"I'll come with you," Kelly offered absently, still watching Amanda without appearing to do so. The other woman was gliding gracefully up to Locke, a red-tipped hand outstretched to put on his sleeve in a bid for his attention.

The disgusting thing was that she got it, Kelly saw unhappily. From across the room it was difficult to follow all of the action, but there was no doubt that her fiancé's dark head was turned downward rather attentively. Kelly thought she saw the banker nod and drift away.

The thing to do with Locke Channing is have an affair but not tie yourself to marriage. Kelly bit her lip. Had Amanda decided to take her own advice, after all? She knew the other woman probably hadn't seen Locke since the broken engagement. Had she walked into the room tonight and remembered belatedly how darkly attractive he could be?

And what had Locke's reaction been after months of not seeing the beautiful hazel-eyed blonde? What memories were going through his head tonight?

"More of our fine-quality jug wine?" Brett teased cheerfully, drawing Kelly's eyes back to himself. He looked at her carefully before pouring. "I wouldn't worry about those two," he said quietly. "They've already decided they're not interested in marrying each other, right? No threat."

"Do I look worried?" Kelly demanded, accepting her glass.

"Let's just say there's a look in your eyes that I never saw there when you and I were dating," he told her ruefully. He lifted his glass in mocking salute. "Here's to your future and mine—even if they aren't meant to be combined."

Kelly hesitated and then lightly clinked her glass against his and sipped the expensive burgundy. She smiled up at him, liking him, even though she knew she could never have loved him. Love was an uncontrollable response to a black-haired, green-eyed warlock. A response that was totally irrational and equally undeniable. She belonged to Locke, she realized a little sadly. He had bound her to him that night he had beaten her at fencing and then made such passionate love to her.

The thought of his lovemaking made Kelly unconsciously glance over her shoulder to find him once again in the crowd. Across the room he looked up from Amanda's glowing face at precisely the same instant, and the green eyes met hers with a strangely shuttered, brooding look. Kelly could feel the hardness in him even though they were separated by several feet and a number of people. Locke was angry.

When he turned back to Amanda, Kelly felt a sharpening anger in herself.

"Listen, Kelly," Brett was saying in a low voice. "What are you going to do about Locke's information? If you can't keep him from going to Helen, then, for God's sake, let me know. It would be far better for her to have the news from me rather than him."

"Don't worry," Kelly said bluntly. "I'll deal with Locke. I think I can persuade him to simply keep quiet about the whole thing. It's the best course of action now. You know that."

"I know it. But it makes me nervous having a third party aware of what's happened."

"He doesn't really know about your involvement. He only knows I fiddled around with the data," Kelly said dismissingly. "He wants to know why but he doesn't seem overly concerned about the ethics of the thing."

"No?" Brett frowned. "I would think, since it's his line of work, that he'd want to impress Helen with the brilliant detective efforts."

Kelly shook her head uncertainly. "Give me a little more time, Brett. I think everything's going to work out. . . . But you could do me a very big favor this evening," she concluded with sudden decision.

"Anything, Kelly. You know that."

"Detach Amanda from my fiancé's arm!"

Brett looked somewhat startled. His blue eyes went speculatively from Kelly's face to the couple across the room. Then he smiled slowly.

"My pleasure. Coming?"

"Of course!" Head regally high, Kelly slipped her arm under his, and together they made their way toward the other two.

The warlock eyes watched her approach, taking in

every detail of Kelly's grip on Brett's arm. She smiled brilliantly at him, enjoying the possibility of his jealousy. Anything to keep his mind off his former fiancée!

It was Brett who, rather surprisingly, took charge of the tense situation.

"There you are, Amanda. I've been looking for you. There's someone I want you to meet, an actor in a local theater guild. I think there's a chance he might want to audition you for that new production they're going to be working on next month."

Amanda's bright-eyed gaze turned immediately on Brett. "Lovely, darling! I would be very happy to meet your friend. You will excuse me, won't you, Locke? It's been fun talking over old times," she added with an amused glance at Kelly's coolly composed features.

She went off without a backward glance, smiling happily up into Brett's good-looking face.

"Enjoying yourself this evening, Kelly?" Locke's words were quite metallic, and the green eyes glowed with an annoyed look that made Kelly feel a little abused. He was the one who had been flirting with an old girl friend!

"Oh, enormously," she assured him in liquid tones. "I found your ex-fiancée quite charming. She gave me all sorts of advice about handling a relationship with you."

"Did she?" he murmured laconically, sipping at his Scotch with a suspended expression on his implacable face.

"Seems to think I'd be better off having an affair with you than marrying you."

He arched one black brow. "I can't see that it matters all that much. One way or the other you'd still belong to me. The wedding vows are a formality."

"A formality you didn't bother going through with Amanda, apparently."

"My relationship with Amanda was altogether different," he began, a dull red staining his neck under the tan.

"Really?" Kelly froze him with her smile. "Does she fence?"

"No!" He nearly exploded, glaring at her. "What's that got to do with anything? And why the hell am I tolerating this inquisition in the first place? You're the one busy renewing a past affair!"

"Oh, Brett?" she said airily, beginning to enjoy herself in a perverse way. There was something exciting about finally finding herself in the right and Locke in the wrong. It satisfied a sense of justice that had been offended the night he'd won the fencing match. "Brett and I are old friends. Why, we weren't even engaged!"

"A state of affairs that is not always a prerequisite for being lovers," he shot back in a thick growl.

"I suppose you would know," she nodded politely, swirling the wine in her glass and sipping delicately.

"I know a great deal about your past relationship with Brett Forrester. Helen told me the two of you used to date very regularly."

"My, you certainly dragged a lot of information out of Helen, didn't you?"

"I like to know the whole picture before I make any changes in the programming."

"A very logical approach," she approved, silver-blue eyes glinting. "But one that apparently didn't work too well when you got engaged to Amanda!"

"Will you stop harping on that subject?" he growled. "I've told you, Amanda was a mistake."

"I didn't think you made them."

"I'm beginning to think I might have made another by not beginning a regular schedule of evening beatings with you. Dammit, Kelly, don't try to make me look like the flirt tonight. You're the one who disappeared to find good old friendly Brett."

"Business," she muttered succinctly.

"Don't hand me that line. What do you think I am? A complete idiot?"

"One wonders occasionally," she agreed. "If you're seriously considering getting involved with Amanda Bailey again—"

"I'm not! And I don't want to hear another word on that subject!" he barked coldly, drawing the attention of a nearby conversation group.

"Mind holding your voice down?" Kelly smiled sweetly. "I can't abide men who make scenes."

"You may damn well have to learn how to put up with them if you're going to continue flirting with old boyfriends," he told her vengefully.

"I was not flirting. I've told you, it was business."

"Tell me about the *business*," he ordered fiercely, dark brows coming together in a solid line above the aggressive nose.

"First why don't you tell me about the 'old times' you and Amanda were discussing?" she challenged, violently aware of the increasing tension between them.

"I will say one thing about Amanda," he snapped instantly. "She never hurled accusations at me in the middle of a party."

"Obviously a woman of insipid spirit!" Her hand was itching to slap his face, Kelly realized with a sense of shock. She'd never slapped a man before in her life!

"You're hardly in a position to criticize my taste when you chose a puppy like Forrester not so long ago yourself!" he bit out.

"Puppies, at least, can be trained," she began seethingly.

"A trained puppy would bore you to death before the honeymoon was over!"

"But one would always know she could *trust* such a creature," Kelly said unthinkingly.

The green eyes froze into emerald ice. "Are you saying

you could trust Forrester and not me?" he asked with appalling civility.

"Brett never threatened me!" she retorted, wishing desperately she hadn't started that particular line of argument. She didn't mean a word of it but she was beginning to feel cornered. It was maddening! Locke was the guilty one, not her!

"That's his error. I won't make the same one."

"I don't see how you could ever expect me to trust a man who continually threatens me."

"You will, nevertheless. And don't blame me if you can't see how that's going to happen. It's not my fault you don't think logically."

"Logically!" Her frustration and anger soared at the word. "Doesn't it occur to you that this whole argument is illogical? You're the guilty one, not me, yet you stand there and act as if I'm a—a—"

"A flirt and a tease?" he supplied grimly. "That's sure as hell the way it looked across the room tonight! And, don't forget, I saw you when you came out of Forrester's office yesterday before lunch. It was obvious something a little more intimate than 'business' had been the topic of conversation!"

Kelly flinched with a touch of guilt. He was right about that, even if he didn't know the full extent of it. Unfortunately she saw at once that he'd seen her guilty start.

With the relentless pressure of a fencer on the attack Locke hammered away at her faltering guard.

"What's the matter, Kelly? Did you discover after you'd met me that you wanted safer men, after all? If you're thinking of rekindling old flames, you can damn well forget it. You belong to me now. You have since the night I beat you on every count."

"Beat me," she snarled softly. "Is that how you see it? Nothing more than a stupid male victory? What makes you think I could possibly be interested in marrying a man

151

who believes he can win a woman by scoring a series of victories over her?"

Another head or two turned speculatively as her voice rose slightly on the last words. Kelly was getting beyond the point where she cared.

"It worked, didn't it?" Locke pointed out with relish. "You *are* going to marry me!"

"What makes you and your ego so damn sure about that?"

"Because I know full well I only have to take you in my arms in order to get whatever I want. That's something Forrester never managed, did he? And you can't have responded like that with any other man because you wouldn't still be single. You would have found yourself locked away with some male's ring on your hand. How does it feel to have met your Waterloo, sweetheart? Or is that what the little flirtation with Forrester was all about? Trying to convince yourself you haven't really met your downfall?"

"One of these days, Locke Channing, you're the one who's going to take a fall. And it will be a pleasure to see you on your knees," Kelly said tightly, her eyes blazing and silver.

"Think of the challenge, darling," he drawled menacingly.

"Oh, I do. Constantly."

"Good. It will give you something to concentrate on," he retorted smoothly, and then added with silky threat, "Because you sure as hell aren't going to concentrate anymore on Forrester or any other man! You've been running wild and free far too long, and I'm going to put a stop to it!"

"Pardon me, but I believe your ego is showing again." Kelly felt that itching sensation in her palm once more. It would be such a pleasure to slap that masculine arrogance out of the green eyes!

"Would you mind very much if we continued this enlightening conversation outside?" Locke asked with mocking politeness, tucking her arm in his in a decidedly savage grip and leading her toward the French doors. In a moment they had passed from the immediate view of others and stood on the balcony.

"I'm freezing!" Kelly snapped, thoroughly irritated.

"Perhaps being a little uncomfortable will cool your temper down a notch! You're behaving like a shrew tonight, Kelly Winfield. I don't like it."

She glared at him. "Pity, because there's not much you can do about it."

"That's a lie and we both know it," he told her coolly, one hand fitting itself to her throat in a vaguely threatening gesture. "Shall I prove it here and now, or would you like to wait until we get home this evening? I can handle you, my sweet sharp-tongued little adversary and I don't mind proving it—"

Whatever he would have said next was lost to posterity because the words were blocked in his throat by the force of Kelly's palm against his tanned cheek.

In the next instant she stifled an astonished gasp of surprise at her own behavior. Never in her life had she lost her self-control like this! She was always the one with the control, always the strong one, the cool one. . . .

She could only stare in wretched amazement as Locke slowly lifted his fingers to the red imprint on his face. There was absolutely no expression at all in the warlock eyes. The eyes of a deadly duelist who gives away nothing to his opponent.

But Kelly didn't need to be able to read his eyes in order to know what would happen next. She was aware of it with every fiber of her being, and a fierce excitement waved through her as she waited for the impact.

When it came, it was so light, she knew Locke was only politely observing the formalities of the duel to which she

153

had just challenged him by the traditional slap. Deliberately he raised his hand and brought his palm across her face in the softest of stinging little slaps.

They stared at each other, ice-blue eyes enmeshed with expressionless green ones, each waiting for the other to say it. It was Locke who finally put it into words.

"My living room or yours?" he asked silkily, daring her to back down.

"Yours, I think," she told him with cool consideration. "Mine is much too small."

He nodded once, reaching out to take her arm in an iron grasp. "You must be very sure of yourself this time. Isn't the memory of your recent defeat still rather close?"

"I know a great deal more about you this time around," she reminded him in a remote and seemingly casual tone. There were traditions surrounding this sort of thing. Opponents must always be cool, horribly polite, and terribly sanguine about the outcome.

"That is, naturally, something of an advantage. One you didn't enjoy the last time," he nodded agreeably. "It will be interesting to see just how much you *have* learned."

His arm firmly entwined around her waist, Locke led Kelly back inside the living room, sought out Helen, and made their apologies for leaving so early.

Kelly thought Helen might raise a protest, but the other woman took one look at the almost frozen expressions on the faces of her two guests and smiled politely.

"I'm sorry you have to leave so soon," she murmured carefully, her sharp gaze on Locke's remote features. "I did mean to ask you if you've set the date of the wedding."

"Next week," Kelly answered, not giving her escort any opportunity to speak.

"So soon?"

"Kelly seems to have a penchant for leaping into dangerous situations," Locke explained easily.

"I'm sure you'll take care of her in this particular situation," Helen offered blandly.

"Yes," he allowed aggressively, "I will!"

With a slight shove that would have appeared more like gentle prodding to an onlooker, he started Kelly toward the door. A moment later they were heading down the stone walk toward where the Jaguar waited by the curb.

"You're sure you want to do this?" Locke asked conversationally, sliding her into the front seat.

"Nothing on this earth could stop me," she promised him fervently.

"I'm glad to hear that," he informed her crisply a second before slamming the door, "because I wouldn't let you out of this match if you got down on your knees and begged!"

"You're the one who's going to be on his knees!"

He shut the door on her fervent promise.

Without a word they drove to her apartment and Locke waited like a leopard for his prey as Kelly collected her foil and fencing garb. When she reappeared in the living room, it was to find him stalking back and forth in front of her window. He glanced up quickly and revealed an astonishingly hungry look that startled her momentarily. Was he *that* eager to gain another fencing victory over her?

In a second the polite, anticipatory mask was back down over his hard face, and she was led briskly back to the car once again.

"It will take me a moment or two to shift the furniture," Locke announced as they walked into his house.

"Fine. I'll go and change." Kelly swept away, feeling the pulsing glow of adrenaline and primitive excitement pounding in her veins. This time would be different! This time she was going to win!

She took her time upstairs in his bedroom, buttoning the fencing jacket with care and adjusting the glove with great attention. Deliberately she forced herself not to think about what had happened in this room after the last fencing bout. Things were going to be different tonight!

She heard him on the stairs and deliberately waited until he had walked down the hall toward the other bedroom before emerging. A few minutes later it was she who waited for him on the field of honor.

"I'd appreciate it if you wouldn't dawdle," she drawled in a fair imitation of a politely bored Regency nobleman awaiting an adversary. "I wouldn't want the horses to get restive."

His answering smile was chillingly appropriate. "Does it occur to you we tend to let our imaginations get a little carried away at this point?" He came down the stairs and crossed the room toward her with a smooth, lithe stride.

She picked up her foil, tucked her mask under her arm, and waited for him to assume his position opposite her.

"My imagination is entirely engrossed with the idea of your defeat," she assured him sweetly.

"Mine, on the other hand, keeps leaping ahead to what happened after our last appointment," he retorted as he picked up his foil. She saw the gleam in the green eyes and stood firm against it. Tonight was *her* night.

"Perhaps you will find the image sufficiently distracting to ruin your concentration," she quipped.

"I think of it as incentive."

He lifted his foil in formal salute and Kelly did the same. Silently they slipped on the masks, retreating behind the deadly anonymity of the wire mesh. It must have been a little different in the old days, Kelly reflected as she came on guard. Looking into the eyes of a man holding an unblunted sword must have added a nerve-wrenching twist to the encounter.

But her imagination was, indeed, working at full power tonight. Because it wasn't difficult at all to think of Locke waiting at dawn for his opponent.

"I see you did learn something the other night," he said as they moved into combat.

Kelly didn't allow herself a self-satisfied smile. Nothing must destroy her concentration tonight. His comment was accurate, however. She was dealing with his aggressive offense with more conviction and sureness this evening. She knew all about his strong wrist and the speed in him.

"You were really spoiling for this fight, weren't you?" Locke chided softly as she made a circular parry to find his blade. "You must have been jealous as hell!"

That drew a response from her in spite of Kelly's firm decision not to allow him to use psychological warfare.

"No!"

Almost instantly she found herself retreating before his foil. Damn him! She would not allow him to get at her like that. She moved swiftly, forcing his words out of her mind, and managed to regain a sense of equality in the match. He parried her attack and she parried his riposte. The action flowed back and forth between them in silence for a time, wariness broken by moments of flashing speed on both sides.

She forced herself to think, knowing that good strategy and uncompromising sureness in the attack were what counted. He *deserved* to lose tonight.

"I'm glad you were jealous, Kelly," he went on after a moment as he closed on her with a quick, sharp blow of his blade against hers. The beat was designed to open a line for his attack by forcing her foil aside for an instant. She barely managed to deceive the action.

"Because I was ready to use my belt on you right there in front of God and Helen!" he went on vengefully.

"Were you jealous, Locke?" she panted, wishing he wasn't forcing her to use so much energy. Kelly was very much afraid her stamina might not hold up against his. Already she could feel the sheen of perspiration on her forehead.

"You know I was, witch! Even when I know I really haven't got anything to worry about, I feel like tearing apart any man who looks at you!"

As if his words gave him impetus, Locke suddenly stopped talking and moved in a lightning-swift series of motions that drove Kelly back nearly to the end of their imaginary mat.

She would not let him get away with defeating her so unfairly again tonight! Furiously she parried and forced her mind to move quickly, her hands reflexively. She needed an edge, or his greater strength and experience would cost her the bout.

"But Brett and I are, after all, old friends . . ." she hissed tantalizingly.

"I'm aware of that."

"Are you?" she taunted, preparing herself for the next split second. She would have to move fast or he would recover before she could land her blow. "Are you aware that Brett is the reason I altered the financial data on the Forrester computer?"

It worked! It worked as thoroughly as his own verbal warfare had done for him during their previous combat, Kelly realized exultantly.

For an instant—a precious instant—Locke's blade faltered. She had taken him completely by surprise. Kelly didn't hesitate. With a fierce, bold lunge she took advantage of his temporary loss of concentration and balance.

Her foil tip plunged, unhindered, toward the target. The score was hers.

CHAPTER TEN

Locke parried and retreated automatically, but it was too late. His foil tip dropped to the floor and with a quick wrench he had the mask off. Jade-green eyes blazed at her as Kelly removed her own mask.

"*Forrester's* the reason?" he nearly shouted, the fury in him radiating toward her like a fire. "Brett Forrester? You risked so much for a puppy like him? I don't believe it!"

"You owe me one more bout," Kelly reminded him coolly, eyeing the anger in him with some trepidation but determined to finish this her way.

"To hell with this game!" Locke shot back. "I want the whole story and I want it now!"

"Then you'd better put your mask back on and give me one more bout."

"I'm not exactly in the mood at the moment," he snapped violently, but there was a wary look in the green eyes and Kelly read it with a certain sense of satisfaction. At long last Locke Channing was beginning to realize what sort of opponent he had taken on when he'd set out to master her!

Kelly traced a small design in the air with the tip of her foil and smiled without saying a word. The tension between them sizzled and it fed her excitement level, stoking the flames ever higher. It was all over. She had known that most of the day. Locke would have his answers tonight—but they weren't going to come for free!

"Don't make me beat it out of you, Kelly," he growled, but he didn't throw down his foil and mask.

"You won't have to exert yourself that much," she drawled, still playing a deadly game with the foil while she waited. "All you have to do is give me one more match. What's the matter, Locke? Too disconcerted to fight with any concentration? Shame on you! A man who's so used to dealing in straight-line logical thought ought to be able to summon up a bit of self-control at a time like this."

"You're serious, aren't you?" he breathed uncomprehendingly. "You drop a bombshell like this into the evening's events and then you expect me to calmly go on with the bout."

"Rather like the night you had your little victory, isn't it?" she agreed smoothly. "As I recall, I was holding my own against you that evening when you dropped *your* little exploding rock into the fray."

"You're doing it this way in order to get revenge?" he asked.

"You've got it in one. You're going to pay for the answers that seem to mean so much to you, Locke Channing," she murmured.

"I could yank that foil out of your hand and turn you over my knee until you begged to be allowed to finish the story!"

"I thought you wanted me to give you the tale voluntarily," she said, chuckling. "You know, as a sign of my trust in you and all that?"

"You are the most annoying, frustrating, stubborn, illogical woman I have ever met in my life," he gritted, sweeping the foil up into the formal salute and snapping on the mask. "And when this is all over, I'm going to take great pleasure in teaching you exactly what your role in life is going to be from now on."

"You're certainly not turning out to be a gracious loser," she mocked as they went on guard.

He said nothing, his fierce concentration directed at putting her immediately on the defensive. Kelly felt the full force of his strength and fencer's stamina as she retreated before the onslaught. He *was* good!

But he was also overeager to end the match. He used his speed and skill well but he didn't vary the cadence of his fighting and Kelly began to find him almost predictable. She knew what he was doing. Locke was going for a quick kill and sacrificing subtlety in the process.

Still, there was a chance that by the sheer force and determination of his attack she would lose the bout. It was unthinkable, Kelly decided as she barely managed to parry in time. Maybe a little more verbal strategy was called for.

"Perhaps I should have said that although Brett was the reason for the computer manipulation," she gasped, panting with the exertion, "I didn't do it for his sake."

"What the devil are you trying to say?" he snarled from behind the mask. As if sensing she was about to hurl another concentration-stopping sally, he tried a stop-hit thrust in an effort to bring the bout to a quick end.

But Kelly was ready for him. Knowing his state of mind, she had deliberately drawn his decisive action with a false attack. Skillfully she parried the stop-hit and the field was open for her counter-time attack.

"Damn!" The stifled exclamation was low, heartfelt, and exceedingly disgusted-sounding. Locke stepped back as the hit landed against his jacket, then he tore off the mask and threw down the foil.

Facing her with his hands on his hips, the black hair tousled and dipping low over his forehead, he waited with unconcealed impatience as Kelly stripped off her mask.

"Don't you dare laugh at me, you little vixen!" he rasped as she grinned boldly across the distance separating them. "When this is all over—"

"No more threats, Locke," she advised tauntingly, silver-blue eyes glittering with satisfaction. He looked every inch the irate warlock standing there ready to pounce, but she knew the moment was hers, and no amount of female caution was going to ruin her victory. "Not if you want the story, that is."

"Talk."

"How does it feel to lose?" she countered cheerfully.

"You've had your little victory," he grated warningly. "I wouldn't advise you to push me too much farther."

"*Little* victory?" she protested. "Hardly little, Locke. I beat you cold. Twice!"

"Using unfair tactics!"

"No more unfair than the ones you used against me the other evening."

He threw up a hand to ward off any more protests. "Okay, okay, I concede utter defeat in the fencing tonight. Does that satisfy you?"

"Yes," she said, pleased with herself. "It does."

"One of these days, Kelly Winfield . . ." he began feelingly.

"Like I said, you're not exactly a gracious loser."

"Let's have it," he ordered briskly, clearly seeing no percentage in further threats at the moment.

Kelly stood silently while she collected her thoughts. The decision to tell him the whole truth had been building since the previous evening. Perhaps, she acknowledged, it had been building since the first day she'd looked into those perceptive green eyes and known she'd met her match.

In a way it would be a relief. The urge to talk to him about the mess had become almost overwhelming. And today, when she'd finally realized she was willing to take the risk of trusting him, she'd known she couldn't deny him his explanation any longer.

But the sense of commitment involved in doing so was strange. Never before had she trusted a man to such an extent. If her instincts were wrong, it would cost her the job at Forrester and, perhaps, a great deal more.

"I want to know every detail, Kelly," Locke said quietly into the silence between them. "Start with Brett Forrester's involvement. I want to know about that most of all."

She stood quietly, watching his implacably set face. Then she plunged into the sordid story.

"Shortly after I arrived at Forrester Stereo, I got involved with that damn computer. There was no way to avoid it in my work. The printouts were becoming a major management tool and I realized I was going to have to learn all I could about the machine and the information coming out of it. So I began studying the manuals and asking questions of the people who do the input work. There was no skilled programmer around at that point to teach me, so I blundered about putting two and two together."

"Exactly what I would have expected of you," Locke muttered in a low tone.

Kelly frowned and then went on. "I began working a lot with the printouts and continually looked over the shoulders of the inputers. I even got to the point where I was doing some of the input and learned how to extract the information from the terminal. Perhaps it was because I was concentrating so much on the thing and getting a solid overview—or maybe because of a coincidence—somehow I picked up on a few discrepancies."

"Discrepancies in what?"

"I was keeping stacks of the old printouts in my office for study purposes. Normally old data was tossed out as the new stuff was cranked out of the computer. When I went back through the old printouts, there were differences in certain areas that I knew shouldn't have existed. Still, I probably wouldn't ever have figured out what was going on if I hadn't also—" Kelly drew a breath. "If I hadn't also begun dating Brett Forrester at that time."

"I'll kill him!" The words were soft, barely audible. Kelly's chin lifted in alarm.

"Don't say things like that. I haven't even finished the story."

"I can guess what comes next."

"Well, don't. You'd probably be wrong."

Locke lifted a shoulder in annoyance. "So tell me," he charged.

Kelly hesitated a second, wondering if she'd made a very serious error in judgment. But she was too far into this now to quit.

"It was obvious Brett was worried about something," she started again, slowly. "I could tell. I also knew he needed to talk about it, and somehow he . . . I—"

"You hit him with a full dose of feminine sympathy and the poor guy instantly cried his heart out on your loving shoulder, right?" Locke sounded grim, and the fury in him was not well leashed.

"He'd got himself into trouble—"

"What sort of trouble? Gambling debts? Fraud? Embezzlement?" The questions came in rapid-fire as if Locke had resumed his blade work.

"Gambling, I gather," she muttered sadly.

"Damn it to hell!" Locke gritted in a disturbingly bleak tone.

"He's stopped now," Kelly heard herself say defensively. "In fact, he'd got scared and stopped before I came on the scene."

"What makes you so sure of that?" he flung back.

"Because what I was turning up in the computer weren't shortages but money being *added* to certain accounts," she snapped, irritated with Locke's lack of sympathy. Brett might not have Locke Channing's strength but he was a good man. . . .

"Are you trying to tell me he was attempting to pay

back the money he'd embezzled?" Locke demanded skeptically.

"Yes."

"But he didn't know how to cover his trail in the computer, right?"

"I could tell from the printout that he was leaving all sorts of holes. Columns of figures that weren't going to add up properly someday, blanks in areas that should have been filled in, a whole bunch of things."

"So he confessed his crime . . ."

"And told me what he was doing to pay back the money."

"And you told him he wasn't covering his trail, right? That someday it was all likely to blow up in his face?" Locke concluded vengefully. He hadn't moved, but Kelly felt as if he were only waiting for the final pounce.

"Not his face. Helen's!"

There was a look of dawning comprehension in Locke's new expression.

"Oh, my God!" he whispered. "You did it for her, is that it? So that she wouldn't have to face the fact that her own son had been stealing company funds?"

Kelly silently nodded. What else could she say? It was the truth.

"Well, thank the Lord for small favors," he intoned gruffly. "Now at least I won't have to tear Brett Forrester limb from limb."

"Locke!" Startled by the implication of what he had just said, Kelly stared at him, horrified.

"Don't look at me like that," he told her tersely. "What else would you have expected me to do if I'd found out you were so much in love with the guy who'd manipulated his mother's accounts?"

"Certainly nothing violent," she retorted angrily.

"Come on now, sweetheart," he mocked. "You know

me better than that. If you were covering up for another man, I'd have done something *very* violent."

"That's a little irrational, isn't it?" she pointed out seethingly. "Not logical at all."

"I've told you we all have our lapses." He brushed aside her next retort. "Tell me something, Kelly. Why were you so willing to protect Helen? You couldn't have known her well at that point."

Kelly shifted her feet and then walked slowly toward the window, gazing out on the lake. It was almost midnight. A duel at midnight, that's what this was. . . .

"Helen gave me a job when I badly needed one. . . ."

"Ah, yes. The sudden move from San Francisco about which you were so reticent."

"You needn't sound as if you were unmasking the villain in the drawing room," she muttered broodingly, her eyes on the lights around the Mercer Island shoreline.

"What happened down there in San Francisco?" he asked quietly.

"There was a man. . . ."

"I figured that much!"

"He thought he was falling in love with me," she went on steadily.

"And he wasn't?" Locke sounded disbelieving.

"He was having trouble with his wife. Only I didn't know about her for some time," Kelly managed in a cool, detached tone. "I only knew that Ward Newlin was having problems. He needed a friend. . . ."

"You're telling me you didn't fall in love with him?" Suddenly Locke sounded very urgent.

She shook her head in a decisively negative answer. How could she fall in love with a man who only needed a friend? "I tried to help him, tried to be the friend and confidante he seemed to need. But something went wrong and he—he began to fall in love with me. He finally told me the whole story, including the fact that he had a wife. I—I felt horrible because I'd gone out with him a few times, let him kiss me—"

"Let him make love to you?" The question was bleak and matter-of-fact.

"No. I didn't love him. I only went out with him because he was lonely."

There was an exclamation of utter disgust from behind her. Kelly ignored it, her fingers tightening at her sides. "He asked me if I would marry him if he left his wife. . . ."

"Wanted to make sure he'd have a woman ready and waiting to take him in before he made the decision to divorce her, is that it?" Locke asked scornfully. "Didn't have the guts to get his own life in order first?"

"You can be a cruel man, Locke," Kelly sighed. "But, yes, essentially that's it. And I finally realized it. I broke off the relationship at once, of course. I wanted no part of breaking up anyone's marriage. But Ward wouldn't leave me alone. He kept coming around, phoning me, sounding distraught. . . ."

"So you started looking for a way out?" Locke hazarded grimly.

"I had been interested in moving to the Pacific Northwest for a long time. California is so crowded, but Washington had always seemed like a young and—and growing place—" She broke off, unable to put the thought completely into words.

"I know," Locke whispered, sounding as if he understood. "So the problems with Newlin seemed like the excuse you needed, is that it?"

"I might not have actually done it. I can handle men like Ward Newlin."

"Having done it before?" Locke guessed accurately enough, sounding wryly amused.

She nodded. "But something happened. His wife got

suspicious and one night she followed him after work. It was just my luck that Ward was making one of his periodic attempts at convincing me we belonged together. He came to my apartment. As soon as I opened the door, his wife appeared. Naturally she assumed the worst. . . ."

"Not without reason, it would seem," Locke reminded her roughly.

Kelly winced. "No, not without reason. I *had* gone out with Ward in the past. And, although I had no intention of ever doing it again once I'd learned about his wife, there was no way she could have known that."

"So what happened next? She threatened to make a scene?"

"Oh, no. She broke down in tears and begged me to leave her husband alone," Kelly said sadly. "I felt like the 'other woman.' It was the most awful experience I've ever been through. I gave her my word there was nothing going on, but Ward wasn't much help. He kept implying things, intimate things. Finally, I was so furious with him, I told them both they wouldn't have to worry about me ever again. I had a job out of the state and I was leaving town."

"Which wasn't altogether true at that point, but the next day you set about making it true, right?" Locke noted dryly.

"Too many people were bound to find out about the situation. People at work, friends, my employer. . . ." Kelly tilted her head to one side, studying the darkness. "I decided there were better things to do with my time than hang around and face all the accusing stares. The Northwest looked very good at that point, job or no job. I'd had it with Ward and the whole scene down there. I opted out."

"And Helen Forrester came through at the opportune moment with a job offer. You, anxious to get away from the scene of your guilt, took flight," Locke finished for her.

Kelly drew a deep, thoroughly annoyed breath. "You

have a way of phrasing things, Locke, that leaves something to be desired."

"It's called being accurate and straightforward," he informed her bluntly.

She didn't bother to reply, aware that he was mulling over what she'd told him. She felt the irritation and impatience in him but she also felt that he believed her. Kelly took great comfort in that, realizing just how anxious she had been even after having made her decision. The relief was incredible.

"So what happens next?" she asked brusquely. "Are you going to clean up my fingerprints in the computer? Or are you going to go to Helen, after all?"

"Is that why you confessed?" he asked with almost clinical interest. "Hoping that if you satisfied my curiosity I'd cover for you and not let Helen know what Brett had done?"

She spun around at that, silver-blue eyes glowing suddenly as she met his warlock gaze. "No," Kelly gritted proudly, tossing her head in a small, haughty gesture. "That's not why I told you. I don't think you would ever have been able to trace the real reasons for my manipulation, would you? You were bluffing when you said you could go back into the computer and figure out the 'why' of the crime."

"That's true," he admitted, sounding genuinely curious. "How did you realize it?"

"The fact that you hadn't done it, I suppose," she said dismissingly. "You're a very thorough man, Locke Channing. You like to make your victories complete. If you knew I'd been manipulating the computer, you wouldn't have stopped at that point. You would have gone on examining the data until you knew why. That night when you . . . when you—" She halted, biting her lip in vexation.

"When I beat you so thoroughly?" he supplied helpfully.

"You would have hit me over the head with the brilliance of your detective work on that score too if it had been possible. You were quite determined to defeat me on every count."

"You're getting to know me rather well," he observed slowly, and for the first time he moved, coming toward her with a lazy, stalking stride.

"You're a lot like me," she whispered, her breath catching in her throat as he reached her and framed her face between two rough palms.

"It took you long enough to realize that," he whispered throatily, gently separating her lips into an inviting pout with his thumbs.

"I think I knew it from the beginning," she husked. "But I couldn't be certain, not after—"

"Not after leaving behind a string of men who weren't at all like you, is that it?" He didn't wait for her answer, finding her mouth with his own and claiming it in a slow, building kiss that demolished the rest of her uncertainties.

It was like finding a harbor after the storm, like accepting the trophy after winning a fencing tournament, like finding the other half of herself, Kelly thought dazedly as she wound her arms around his neck and gave herself up to the delight of Locke's embrace.

"My sweet little adversary," he muttered thickly, moving his lips searchingly over hers and sliding his hands down to her shoulders. "I've been waiting for you all my life, did you know that?"

"I only know I've been waiting just as long," Kelly breathed. "Love me, Locke, please love me. I love you so very much. . . ."

His fingers went to the buttons on the fencing jacket, undoing the top buttons so that he could slide his hands lightly around her throat and then to her waist. They stood close together, cradled in each other's arms.

"I loved you the moment I walked through your office

170

door," Locke told her softly. "I took one look at you and knew I'd met the woman I'd go to hell and back in order to have. The only problem lay in convincing you that you were meant for me."

"When you walked in, I saw the man who could ruin every one of my fine plans. The man I had been half hoping, half fearing existed. I told myself that the excitement and attraction I felt were based on the danger involved. But that wasn't it at all. I was falling in love and I didn't recognize the symptoms."

With a swift, powerful movement Locke stooped and lifted her into his arms, smiling down into her face as she looked up at him. Her fingers went to the nape of his neck, kneading the strong muscles there and thrilling to the feel of his thick dark hair.

The heat and scent of their bodies were enhanced by the dampness generated by the combat exertions. Kelly inhaled the strong masculine fragrance and felt her pulse increase.

Gently Locke settled her on the couch, coming down on top of her and crushing her deeply into the cushions.

"We're going to be married just as soon as I can arrange things," he told her positively, stroking her temples with his fingertips. "I can't bear to let you out of my sight!"

"Afraid I'll get into more trouble?" she teased, arching herself languidly against him and glorying in his immediate response.

He moved one hand down her body, stroking the shape of breast and hip and thigh with loving possessiveness. "I don't think you'll be getting into any more of your usual man-trouble," he grinned, looking far too sure of himself.

"No?"

"No. You're mine now, aren't you? You've been mine since the night I made you eat your Waterloo in one gulp. And you proved it tonight when you finally told me the full truth about that computer caper. Lord knows I've been wanting to hear that explanation!"

"Why? Afraid it might have been worse than it was?" she teased, enjoying the long stroking actions of his hand. She felt like a sleek cat being petted. "What would you have done if it turned out I *had* been embezzling from Forrester?"

"Married you anyway," he grinned unrepentantly.

"You know, I've had a few serious doubts about your own business ethics lately," Kelly accused with a laughing grimace. "You never did seem unduly worried about the rights and wrongs of the situation, only about my role in it and getting me to admit it."

"That's all that mattered to me. I wouldn't have altered my course of action if I'd discovered you'd also been behind that inventory problem or a dozen other illegal activities. I took one look in your eyes and knew there had to be a good reason for your actions. I was determined to make you confess it and, in so doing, prove you trusted me that much at least."

"I trust you, Locke," she admitted with sudden serious conviction. "I knew almost from the beginning that you were going to play a major role in my life. You *understood* things about me that no other man has ever understood. And I knew from the start that I wasn't going to have to feel sorry for you. It was myself I should be saving my sympathy for!"

"True enough," he agreed with a warning smile playing about the sensuously hard line of his mouth. "I'm going to change your whole life and you're going to change mine."

His mouth came back down on hers and simultaneously his body pressed against hers, his legs moving aggressively between hers. She didn't resist, but welcomed him close with loving arms. The electricity and warmth raced through her body, inciting the longing and passion that

172

seemed to hover so close to the surface when he touched her.

"My darling Kelly," he breathed on a note of rising passion as he rained kisses on her face and throat. He groaned hoarsely as she twisted catlike beneath him. "I love you so much."

"I love you. Oh, Locke, we were so very lucky to find each other. . . ."

"Luck, hell!" he rasped, his lips on the small bones of her shoulder as he undid the white shirt at the collar. "I fought for this, my lovely adversary. Luck had nothing to do with it."

"Whatever you say," she said in a husky, sultry tone, her fingers clinging to the thrusting curve of his wide shoulders. "Whatever you say."

For a time there was only the heated exchange of their bodies as they tasted and drank of each other. Pressed as tightly together as it was possible to be while still clothed, they gave unstintingly of their passion and love.

Blissfully Kelly sighed, waiting for the moment when Locke would finish the task of undressing her and completing their union. Before this his lovemaking had been a way of binding her to him. Tonight it would be a seal on their feelings for each other.

His hands moved on her and his mouth trailed liquid fire across her skin. But he made no effort to undress her. Perhaps he didn't want to rush her, Kelly thought, full of warmth at the prospect of Locke trying to temper his urgency for her sake. But it wasn't necessary. Not tonight. Couldn't he tell she wanted him as badly as he wanted her?

She surged upward against him, a low moan of deep feminine invitation catching in her throat. She slid her hands lovingly along his back and around to the front of his jacket, searching for the buttons. If he was waiting for a sign of her readiness, she would give it to him.

Her hands had barely begun the task when he quickly seized them in one large fist and carefully pulled them over her head, out of reach of his shirt fastenings.

"Oh, no, you don't, sweetheart," he vowed with a shaky little laugh. "I'm not going to let you ruin all my good intentions, little wanton!"

"Locke! What are you talking about?" she gasped, torn between humor and passionate desire. Silvery eyes wide, she searched the warlock gaze for an explanation.

"You set me up as the watchdog, remember?" he taunted lovingly, trailing the tip of his finger down the line of her cheek and jaw. "Before we left for the party this evening, you made it plain that you didn't have the will-power to resist me, that you were going to have to trust me to call a halt to our lovemaking."

"But, Locke, that's not necessary now. I love you and—and you've said you love me. . . ." Horrified at the prospect of not spending the night telling him with her body how much he meant to her, Kelly could only stare, transfixed.

"I think it's very necessary," he whispered with an amazing degree of masculine will. "I've used sex as another weapon to gain my victories and I think it's time I demonstrated that I've got some inner fortitude! I want you to remember always that, in the final analysis, you really can trust me. About everything!"

"You're going to send me home tonight?" she whispered, shocked, but comprehending what he was trying to do.

"I'm going to take you home and then I'm going to give you a proper courtship," he promised arrogantly, sitting up slowly and releasing her. "I'm going to show you that I know how to woo a woman with other means than swords and sex!"

"Oh, Locke." Unable to stifle the laughter, Kelly gave in to it, shaking her head in rueful exasperation. "Why bother with the hearts and flowers when the swords and sex were so successful?"

"You've got a point there." He grinned. "I guess it's the romantic in me."

"The romantic?" For a split second Kelly was dazed by that thought and then she smiled with sudden understanding. "You've already proven how much of a romantic you really are, Locke Channing, don't you know that?"

He eyed her with a curiously wary, slanting glance. "Is that so?"

"Oh, yes." She smiled cheerfully, reaching out to touch his arm with love and understanding. "Did you think you could hide behind your computer console? I've known you were a romantic from the beginning. It seems to be something other people don't always see in you, however."

"Other people like Amanda Bailey?" he demanded dryly, not arguing about her conclusion. "I should explain about that, I suppose."

"You don't have to."

He shrugged. "Might as well. Amanda was a mistake. I've admitted I make them occasionally. She's very attractive and I thought—I don't know exactly what I thought. Something about companionship and sex and having a wife before I got too much older." He shook his head in self-directed annoyance. "I realized almost immediately I'd made a huge error. But it wasn't Amanda's fault and I couldn't just dump her. . . ."

"So you buried yourself in your work and proved what a dull, uninteresting, and utterly boring husband you would be, hmmm?" Kelly smiled again.

"It worked. It was a tremendous relief for both of us when we split up. I gave myself a good scare that time and decided I would have to be very careful about relationships in the future. Then you entered my life and I realized I wouldn't have to be at all careful with my relationships. For you I was going to throw caution to the wind!"

"A true romantic!"

"You really think so?" He grinned.

"I knew it the moment I saw those foils on your wall. I remember looking up and seeing them and telling myself that it was okay to go to war with you because you *understood!*"

"Oh, I understood, all right," Locke admitted gently as she sat up beside him on the couch. "I understood I had to have you no matter what the cost. I've never felt like that about any woman before in my life. It was almost frightening. Frightening and exciting and exhilarating, and there was no alternative."

"Like meeting an adversary on a grassy clearing at dawn with a sword in your hand?" she suggested.

"And with no safety mask or blunted tip," he added with a smile.

Kelly smiled back at him as they faced each other with complete understanding.

"I think," Locke said with great control, "that I'd better get you home before I let those silver-blue eyes destroy my good intentions."

She saw the longing in his face, felt it in his touch when he reached for her hand. She glanced down at his loose grip on her wrist and opened her palm upward in a delicate, vulnerable gesture.

Locke traced an unbelievably erotic pattern there and then lifted her hand and kissed the sensitive area. Without a word he pulled her to her feet and headed for the door to where the Jaguar waited outside.

"Does it strike you," Kelly said quite seriously on her doorstep before he turned to go, "that we're both a bit lacking in what are termed conventional moral principles?"

"Not our fault," he assured her with a slow, affectionate smile. "People like us sometimes have to make our own."

In the darkness of her brass-trimmed living room Kelly

closed the door and reflected on the knowledge that she and Locke had no need to worry about each other's weaknesses because they knew and understood each other's strengths.

CHAPTER ELEVEN

Kelly emerged from the bathroom on her wedding night to find Locke waiting for her. He was wearing a cotton toweling robe, carelessly tied around his narrow middle. The gun-metal hair was still damp from the shower and the loosely bound robe revealed a great deal of more dark hair on his chest. He glanced up from the piece of paper in his hand and smiled.

Kelly felt his eyes rove over her in love and desire, and the warmth washed through her veins. She stood for a moment, outlined by the light behind her, and contemplated her husband.

How she loved him, she thought wonderingly. More than she had ever thought she could love any man. She watched the green eyes drink in the sight of her supple body as it gleamed through the sheer copper satin of her nightgown and heard him draw in his breath.

"I don't know how I waited until tonight," he ventured finally, not moving. "I've spent the past few nights gazing at my ceiling and thinking that I'd never make it. I want you so badly, my sweet wife. I won't ever be able to get enough of you."

Kelly shivered under the ardent gaze and tried to construct a light reply. The atmosphere in the room was already very heavy with leashed passion waiting to be set free.

"Are you sure you didn't marry me just to gain a per-

178

manent fencing partner?" She smiled, coming slowly forward.

"Honey, I would have married you if you didn't know one end of a foil from the other!" he declared fervently, his eyes sweeping her figure and coming back to settle on her face.

Kelly knew she was trembling and tried to control her overpowering reaction to her warlock. "What's that in your hand?" she whispered, glancing at the single sheet of computer paper.

"This? It's your wedding present." He handed it to her.

Confused, Kelly glanced at the brief series of notations. At the top of the page was a date and the password she used when accessing the computer.

"It's beautiful," she said, grinning at him. "And just what I've always wanted. What is it?"

"Something tells me you've got a lot to learn about computers—in spite of your light-fingered romp through the Forrester data base. That, my dearest wife, is a record of all the transactions you made on the computer during the period you were making your 'corrections.' "

Kelly's brows drew together again as she glanced back at the few lines of computer print. "But this shows I only went in half a dozen times. I must have gone in dozens of times."

"About a hundred and fifty," he acknowledged dryly, watching her in amusement.

"But this only shows six or seven."

"That's all the computer now has a record of," he murmured.

"Oh," she said a little weakly. "I see. You've altered the record. Cleaned up my fingerprints in the Fortran?"

"Ummm. I left a few entries there so that if anyone ever did happen to go looking he wouldn't find a suspicious *lack* of them. Everyone knows you've spent plenty of time on the machine. It would look strange if there was a complete blank for a certain period. Not," he went on reassuringly, "that anyone is ever likely to do so. You did a pretty good job of changing the data."

"I just didn't know enough to alter the record of my having been in and out of the data base, is that it?" Kelly asked ruefully.

"I'm afraid so." He waited and she had the feeling she hadn't fully acknowledged her gift.

With a touch of uncertainty she glanced back at the paper in her hand and her eyes fell on the date this particular piece of paper had been generated on the printer.

"But, Locke!" she exclaimed disbelievingly. "You ran this before we had that first dinner out together. The second day you were at Forrester!"

"Yes."

"You cleaned up the record as soon as you found it?" she squeaked, astonished. Her eyes lifted to his and she thought she would melt under the green fire she saw there.

"I didn't want to take the slightest chance that someone else would stumble across what I'd discovered. It seemed safest to take care of your little fingerprints as quickly as possible."

"But you told me you could go to Helen and show her what had been happening. You wouldn't have had any proof."

"I never intended to go to Helen, you sweet idiot. My first instinct was to protect you and then find out what the hell was going on in the data base."

"Oh, Locke!" Dropping the paper on the nightstand, she ran into his arms, taking pleasure in the solid support she found as she landed with an impact.

His arms came around her and she nestled against his chest with total confidence and love.

"Thank you," Kelly whispered, "for having that sort of faith in me."

"Don't you understand, Kelly?" he growled hoarsely

into the soft hair that hung down her back. "I would have protected you if you'd been guilty of stealing a fortune from Helen. But my instincts told me there were reasons for what you had done. You're too proud, too self-sufficient, to have lowered yourself to theft."

"Too much like you?" she teased, lifting her fingertips to the tanned base of his throat and trailing them lightly down the bare chest.

"I guess so." He grinned, his hands sliding down her waist, relishing the slick feel of the copper satin against her skin. "Besides, it's all over, anyhow. Brett paid back the money and from what you've said he won't be getting into that sort of trouble again."

"No, he's learned his lesson. Had learned it before I came along, really. And I've convinced him there's no point in getting it off his conscience. Helen would be shocked. It's not worth hurting her."

"No."

"I'm sorry I don't have a proper wedding gift for you," Kelly murmured.

"Oh, but you do," he teased, his palms slipping down over the curve of her buttocks and cupping the flesh with possessive urgency. "And it's one you can keep on giving me, over and over again. . . ."

"I knew it," she sighed, her body pressing more closely into his hardness. "You just wanted a built-in fencing partner."

"I suppose you could call it that," he agreed, nuzzling the skin at the nape of her neck beneath the cascade of red and gold highlighted hair. "There certainly are some similarities."

She trembled at his meaning and chained her arms around his neck, raising her face for his kiss. The sensuous twining of her body against his aroused him fiercely and she was incredibly aware of the hard male need in him.

Locke used his hands to propel her hips intimately

against his, leaving her in no doubt about the level of his desire, and Kelly moaned softly in response.

"My sweet Kelly," he husked, sliding the straps of the copper gown from her shoulders and slipping it lovingly down her body to form a pool on the floor. "I want you so much. You'll never know how hard it's been for me the past few days."

He lifted her out of the copper pool and carried her to the turned-down bed, then set her down in the middle. For a moment he simply gazed down at her with a hungry green fire in his eyes that made her feel wanted, needed, and loved. It also excited her beyond reason.

"You only have to look at me and I don't seem to have any resistance," she admitted, shaking her head as he shouldered himself out of the toweling robe and came down beside her.

"Do you want to resist?" he mocked, his hands encircling the tips of her high, thrusting breasts. He bent to kiss each nipple in turn and then smiled down at her.

"There was a time when I thought I did," she admitted. "But even then—"

"It's impossible to resist someone who was made for you. Ask me, I know!"

"For a man who's spent most of his adult life around computers, you have an amazing grasp of the more basic human emotions," she murmured admiringly, spearing her fingers through the blackness of his hair.

"I've been studying hard while waiting for you to appear in my life so that I could test out my theories!"

"Pleased with the results?"

"Very!"

He began to move his hands on her body in possessive little forays that coaxed and excited. Kelly felt every inch of her skin come alive under his touch and she returned the passionate caresses with all the ardor of her strong, deeply sensitive nature.

But it was only with Locke that the strength and passion could be fully released, she realized dimly as the caresses grew more inviting. He understood it, just as she understood him. Together they could be themselves in a way it would never be possible to be with others.

She had found a man whose strength matched her own. One who could be relied upon and one who could rely on her. The pact they had made was going to be binding forever and they each knew it.

"I made you my woman that first time I took you to bed," Locke grated heavily as he kissed the skin of her shoulder. "Tonight I will make you my wife."

"Is there a difference?" she husked, her breath beginning to come in short pants of mounting desire. "I knew I belonged to you that night. I don't think I could have ever escaped that knowledge, even if you had walked out of my life then and there or turned me over to Helen."

"I forged a two-way bond that night," he admitted thickly. "I was chaining myself to you as thoroughly as I was tying you to me. But, yes, there is a difference between then and tonight. Tonight you're my *wife!* Tonight we seal the bond."

And then he demonstrated the full scope of the passion that flared between them, making love to Kelly with a power and grace that left her breathless and writhing beneath him.

"Oh, Locke! Locke!"

His name was the only coherent sound she could manage as he turned her body to flame beneath him. His hands brought her to the brink of the dazzling universe he had shown her twice before, and when they stepped inside, she knew the full force of the power they generated together.

"Love me, sweet wife," he begged hoarsely. "Love me forever!"

Kelly responded, clutching him to her with small moans of pleading desire. She thought she would go crazy if he didn't claim her completely, so aroused was she by the intimate caresses and the rough male feel of his body on hers.

And then, when she thought she could not stand another moment of his loving, exciting hands and lips, she was aware of his naked thighs on hers, his hands touching the inside of her leg with persuasive, insinuating designs. A moment later he was arching into her softness, claiming her once again on the most primitive and timeless of planes.

She clung and clung and clung, her nails sinking wildly into the strong muscles of his back and waist and then his taut thighs. She followed the cadence of his sensual fencing, not retreating before his passionate onslaught, but absorbing him into her in the ultimate sort of victory.

"Kelly! My own! My wife!"

The cry was torn from him as she shivered violently in his arms, and in the next instant he was joining her in the endless culmination of their passion. Together they clung through the whirling triumph of their emotions, guiding each other, loving each other, and cementing their relationship with the elemental force of their need and love.

It was a long time before Kelly stirred sleepily in her husband's arms. Lazily, sensuously, she stretched, deliberately letting her high-tipped breasts touch his chest as she turned on her side to meet his eyes.

Propping her chin on her hands, she smiled at Locke, the silver in her eyes still molten. He smiled back, jade gaze glinting with warmth and love.

"It's absolutely amazing," she drawled provocatively, "what sort of liberties the hired help takes these days!"

"Nonsense," he contradicted chidingly. "It's not all that uncommon to marry the boss."

"I'm pleased you still remember the relationship between us. I thought that you might have got ideas above your station after putting a wedding ring on my finger!"

"I resent the implication that I don't know my place." He grinned, twisting his fingers in her tousled hair. "After all, I was quite aware of it from the beginning. You were the one who took a little educating!"

"Think I've learned the lesson?" she murmured hopefully.

"I expect I'll have to repeat it regularly, but that's all right. I have nothing else to do during the evenings. I've never been much of a socializer. We'll stay home and practice fencing in front of the fire, and after that we'll practice making love." He broke off. "That reminds me. . . ."

"I know." She giggled. "You're hungry, right?"

"We all have our little quirks," he agreed blandly.

"If we do this often enough, we'll get fat," she pointed out.

"Life is not without its little risks," he told her philosophically, "Besides, we need to fortify ourselves for the rest of the night. A good dose of protein should hit the spot."

"Whatever you say," she agreed, swinging her feet over the edge of the bed and reaching down to pick up the copper gown. She slid it over her head and eyed him suspiciously. "You're not moving very quickly for someone on his way to satisfy a quirk."

"I was just thinking," he drawled, his hands behind his head as he watched her avidly. "Perhaps I should practice trying to break the habit."

She smiled down at him. "I wouldn't want you to go hungry."

"No, but I could try postponing the protein for a bit, say until after I've made love to you twice instead of once."

"I wouldn't want to be the cause of you changing any

185

lifelong habits," Kelly told him cheerfully and made for the door.

He was off the bed and had her high in his arms before she quite realized what had happened. Purposefully he carried her back and dumped her lightly down on the rumpled sheet.

"You're the most addictive thing in my life now," he told her throatily, kissing the smooth skin of her shoulder with lingering relish.

"Yes," she said simply, achingly. "Yes. I know what you mean."

VOLUME I IN THE EPIC NEW SERIES

The Morland Dynasty

The FOUNDING

by Cynthia Harrod-Eagles

THE FOUNDING, a panoramic saga rich with passion and excitement, launches Dell's most ambitious series to date—THE MORLAND DYNASTY.

From the Wars of the Roses and Tudor England to World War II, THE MORLAND DYNASTY traces the lives, loves and fortunes of a great English family.

A DELL BOOK $3.50   #12677-0

Dell Bestsellers